SISTERS OF THE CRIMSON VINE

P.L. MCMILLAN

Timber Ghost Press

Copyright © 2022, P.L. McMillan

Published by Timber Ghost Press

Printed in the United
States of America

Edited by: Beverly Bernard

Front Cover Art and Design by: Donnie Goodman at Atonic Vision Designs

Back Cover Art by: P.L. McMillan

Back Cover Design by: M. Halstead

Interior Design: Timber Ghost Press

Print ISBN: 979-8-9855521-4-0

Digital ISBN: 979-8-9855521-3-3

LCCN: 2022945072

Praise for *Sisters of the Crimson Vine*

"A taut braid of repressed desires, implied deviance, and eldritch horror. McMillan coyly lures us to a finale as repulsive as it is compelling."
– Stoker award-winning Jamie Flanagan, co-writer of *The Haunting of Bly Manor* and *Midnight Mass*

"In her masterful debut novella, *Sisters of the Crimson Vine*, P.L. McMillan cultivates dread like a fine wine. The more we sip, the deeper we sink into this insidious tale grown from the seed of Jackson's "The Lottery" planted in a Lovecraftian terroir and harvested in Ari Aster's *Midsommar*. Like the title characters' famed libation, you will not be able to stop reading once you imbibe. A drunken sense of imbalance and uncertainty remains with you until the very end. Lovers of the occult will be pleasantly satiated by P.L. McMillan's gothic offering."
– Stoker award-winning EV Knight, *Three Days in the Pink Tower*

"*Sisters of the Crimson Vine* by P.L McMillan is folk horror at its very best. The visuals, tension and mood created then intermixed with undeniable dread and mystery rides the very edges of illumination and darkness. P.L explores themes of religious hypocrisy and the power of women and sacrifices made to survive. She expertly subverts older tropes into something terrifying and new. This book is as vivid and twisted as any Aster movie." – Brenda S. Tolian, *Blood Mountain*

"*Sisters of the Crimson Vine* is a perfectly paced suspenseful story that will make you want to savor every word. Invoking the ominous folk horror atmosphere of the *Wicker Man* and *Midsommer*, P.L. serves an unsettling tale of the supernatural bond between women and nature and the power and price of living free from patriarchal dominance." – Joy Yehle, author and host of *The Burial Plot* horror podcast

Contents

Dedicated to Mom and Dad
For exposing me to horror when I was young
and being my faithful cheerleaders now

PART I

Harvesting

I tugged at the corner of my road map, trying to open it further as it lay across my passenger-side seat. The bumpy country road spun ahead of me through the fields, dips, and rolling hills. I glanced back down at the map again, wondering where I'd taken the wrong turn. Looking up at the road, I saw a deer out in the middle of my lane, staring at my car with a blank, stupid gaze.

I reacted—poorly to say the least—by yanking on the steering wheel. The car's wheels ground the dirt, spitting stones out in a rooster tail as the car's rear swung out in a wild arc. Spinning off the road, I jerked at the steering wheel, trying to correct.

The front bumper caught the ditch at a bad angle. Everything tipped. My head slammed against the car door, exploding stars across my vision. Momentum spun me and my car over and over, out of the ditch and through the wild grass in the neighbouring field. The windshield shattered with a dull crack. I shut my eyes, gripping the steering wheel hard. Spinning in darkness, a final impact and my head struck the wheel, piercing my brain with bright, white pain.

Waking up came in stages. First an awareness of pain, constriction across my chest, difficulty breathing.

Next, a rising, slow and difficult, as if from mud. A hint of light, and I opened my eyes, unfocussed, vision wandering. Pain chased my thoughts, scattering them so that it took me a while before I realized that I was upside down.

That my car, in fact, was upside down, crumpled enough that the top of my head rested against the ruined roof.

The seatbelt dug into my chest and shoulder and I struggled with the buckle, but it wouldn't give. Reaching for the steering wheel, I pushed myself against the seat. The belt slackened and I reached for the buckle, releasing it.

I crumpled to the roof of my car, moaning as my head thundered in agonized response. My arms lay pinned underneath me and I squirmed to roll onto my side, bracing my feet against the top of the passenger-side seat. My stomach rolled in the opposite direction and, before I could swallow it back, I vomited onto the fabric that lined my car's roof.

Over the wretched smell of my partially digested breakfast, I caught an acrid whiff of petrol. Fear shot through me, clearing my mind abruptly. My car was leaking petrol. I pushed myself onto my hands and knees, only noticing for a brief moment how my left leg shrieked before I began to drag it, and myself, out the shattered windshield.

The remaining shards of glass, still jutting out from the windshield frame, sliced through my palms, my knees, my shins, as I pulled myself out of my car and onto the grass. I grabbed fistfuls of the parched plants and dragged myself farther and farther from my car, all the while waiting for it to burst into flames or explode. My left leg followed uselessly behind, refusing to help.

I had a vague idea that I should get to the side of the road so that a passing motorist might see me and be able to help. Around me, the land swam, the sky and trees whipped round and round. My stomach clenched and I retched, my whole body heaving as only a few foul-tasting strings of bile dripped from my lips.

My head throbbed, pain pounding in my ears like thunder. I curled up, reached for my head and felt something hot and sticky coat my hands.

I squinted in the dimming light—was my vision fading, or had the day disappeared while I had lain unconscious in my car?—and saw my palms smeared with blood.

I heaved myself back onto my hands and my single working knee. My vision narrowed, focussed on the ground beneath my hands, and I concentrated on moving, always moving, trying to find help. Crawling for minutes, hours, seconds, eternity, I didn't find the road. All I heard was the throbbing of my blood in my ears, all I smelled was my own vomit, and my vision darkened further until I saw nothing at all but crimson flashes matching the tempo of the pain in my skull.

I was lost in pain. My arms shook, gave in, I sunk to the ground. For a moment, I told myself. For just a moment's break. A rest.

The next time I opened my eyes, I was looking up at a white ceiling with cracked paint. My whole body trembled and a sick heaviness weighed on me, suffocating me.

I fought the fatigue. I lost.

The time after that, I opened my eyes, and the white ceiling was wreathed with shadows. Somewhere distant, I heard voices. A man's raised voice and a woman's soft responses. The fugue that hung over my mind like stubborn fog cushioned me. There was no pain, only a sense of detachment. Sleep stole over me and I welcomed it.

When I woke next, things were clearer, and not only because the sun had returned, flooding the room with light. My body ached and my head still echoed with the remnant of a receding headache, but I was back, fully back again to my senses.

Lifting my hands, I brought them above my face where I could see them. Clean gauze wrapped my palms and fingers. I bent my fingers a bit to test them and flinched at the sharp stabs of pain that lanced through both hands, making me gasp.

The pain helped me remember. My desperate crawl through the glass of my windshield, the reek of petrol, the fear. I flinched at the phantom pain of glass slicing through my skin, my flesh.

Delicately, I touched my neck, cheeks, forehead, top of head. The memories trickled back, as if activated by my sparking pain receptors. My heart kicked up a notch in my chest and I breathed out a long sigh, the relief mixing with the aching of my head. I'd been found. I'd been found by someone and brought to... not a hospital, somewhere else.

When the relief faded back, I was overwhelmed with thirst. My dry throat clicked whenever I swallowed; my tongue lay thick and gluey at the roof of my mouth. The idea of struggling to get out of bed, to walk and find water, a tap, anything, was daunting, exhausting.

"Glad to see you awake, Mr. Ainsworth." A woman appeared at my side.

I stared at her, my jaw hanging open, but she seemed to take no notice. Or more likely, as suggested by the nature of her clothing, she was kind enough to pretend not to see. For this woman was dressed in the traditional black garb of a nun. One thing that stood out was the fact that she wore no wimple. Her blonde hair hung in a neat braid over her shoulder, tied with some string. More importantly, she was carrying a tray with a pitcher, bowl, and glass.

She set the tray down somewhere beside me and I tried to push myself into a seated position, only to be discouraged by how my hands reacted to the pressure. I must have gasped because the nun was at my side in an instant, firm hands on my shoulders.

"You shouldn't try to move too much on your own, Mr. Ainsworth." She bent over me, hooking her hands under my armpits, and lifted me. "You were rather lucky that Mr. Hall found you when he was out for his morning walk in his fields, otherwise you may not have made it at all."

She was efficient, holding me up while arranging the pillows behind me. Despite how thin she seemed to be, she still held me with ease, with a strength I wouldn't have expected.

Carefully, she settled me back on the pillows, propped up enough that I could see about the room easily.

The room was long, containing several beds besides the one in which I lay. All the beds were pushed up against the inner wall, allowing any occupants to gaze out of the small windows on the opposite wall. These windows went down the length of the room, allowing a large amount of natural light to stream in. Each bed had its own side table; mine was now laden with the tray brought in by the nun.

She picked up the pitcher and filled the small glass with water. As gentle as she would with a child, she held it to my lips and watched with a smile as I sucked down greedy gulps. Once the glass was half empty, she took it from me, setting it back onto the tray.

"You were in quite a state when he brought you in. Face, neck, and hands coated in blood. Your left leg was bent at an atrocious angle, Sister Morgan May practically fainted at the sight of you!" the nun said, stifling a laugh behind one pale hand.

"My leg?" I asked, a memory of pain creeping in.

I tried to move my left leg and found it heavy, awkward. The nun placed a hand on it to still my movements and I didn't feel her touch at all.

"Don't worry," she said. "I have some medical experience and, with help, was able to put it right. You won't be walking on it today, though."

She knocked her knuckles against my leg and I felt a slight vibration through the plaster.

"Where am I?" I asked.

The nun turned to the table, picking up the small bowl.

"You're at the Crimoria Convent and I am Sister Helena Rose," she said, and held the lip of the bowl to my lips.

I took a sip. The bowl was full of lukewarm broth, pleasantly herbed and salty. I drank it down, trying not to slurp in front of the nun, realizing how hollow my stomach felt. Once the bowl was empty, Sister Helena Rosa put it back on the tray. Having now had something to eat and drink, I felt more grounded, more situated.

"How did you know my name?" I asked her.

Helena smiled then, a playful kind of smile, altogether not something I'd expect to see on the face of a nun, and she reached down to pull open the drawer of the side table next to my bed. From the drawer, she retrieved a small leather wallet, familiar to me despite the new dark stains on it.

"I cleaned it as best I could, but blood is difficult to remove from leather," she said, putting it back and closing the drawer.

A drowsiness draped over me like a comfortable blanket and I felt my eyelids droop with the weight. The nun bustled around me, rearranging the pillows again to allow me to lie back fully. I closed my eyes and listened to her pick up the tray and walk away.

I woke up sometime later when the bright sunlight had mellowed into a softer evening orange. My stomach growled. Despite Sister Helena's previous rebuke, I pushed myself up onto the pillows and into a seated position with only a few moments of pain. From this position, I could command a better view of the outside through the window across the room from me.

Directly outside was a small copse of trees, beyond that were rolling fields. Both the woods and fields showed the effects of the summer's unseasonable heat and lack of rain. Where the trees should be a deep green, they were rather more washed out looking, and the grass was yellowed, as if the sun had baked all the colour from them. The fields should have been growing thickly with whatever crops the farmers had planted, but were gray and barren. Beyond the copse of trees, I could see the peaked roofs of a nearby village. Evidently, I had been lucky enough to crash my car close to civilization.

I looked about the room. It seemed to be a dormitory, or maybe even a ward, but currently I was its only occupant. Though it was clean, I could clearly see that it was rundown. The plaster on the ceiling was chipped in places, discoloured in others—the largest being a dark water stain at the farthest corner.

The sheets I was lying under were clean but stiff, cheap feeling. In many places, I could see where holes had been worn through and then carefully repaired with tight stitching.

My stomach growled again and I wondered how I was supposed to get help. There was no bell on the bedside table, or phone, and around me was only silence. In fact, I looked around the room again to be sure. There was no sign of working electricity at all, no overhead lights or lamps, no fans to chase away the oppressive heat, or radiators for when winter finally came.

Besides my hunger, I felt how heavy my bladder was. I tossed the blankets off and stared down at the thick, rough cast on my leg. My face grew hot as I imagined poor Sister Helena trying to deal with holding a bedpan for me or helping me on and off a toilet. Rolling to one side of the bed, I looked over the edge. Peeking out from beneath was the rim of a small ceramic bowl.

I stared at it for a good minute.

A chamber pot.

"Oh man," I said to myself, to the empty room, to the chamber pot.

Regardless, I knew I needed to take care of the pressing matter and I pulled the pot out from under the bed. Lying on my side, the next few moments of my life were an awkward balancing act.

I had just finished when I heard footsteps. Desperate not to be caught out in the open by a woman of God—I had flashbacks of the ruler-happy nuns of the Catholic school I'd attended—I tucked the bowl back under the bed and yanked the blankets back over me.

The footsteps continued to approach before finally stopping in front of the closed door to my room. The door opened and Sister Helena Rose was the first one in, a smile on her face. Behind her, closely following, was a man. He was a short, stout man, balding and with reddened jowls. His eyes were small, set close together, and seemed cruelly observant. He was dressed in a black cassock with the standard white collar of a Catholic priest.

The nun approached and set a tray down on the table next to me. Noticing the blankets I had rumpled, Helena tucked them back tightly around my legs and sides.

"Mr. Ainsworth, I'm glad to see you up! I've brought your dinner and an esteemed guest," she said.

"Hello, Father," I said, eyeing the bowl of broth.

"Father Griffith," the man said in reply, his hands clasped behind his back as he walked down the length of the room, bending to peek beneath beds and out of windows.

"Father Griffith is visiting from London," Helena said, bringing the bowl to my lips.

I cared more for satisfying my stomach than making friends, so I gulped the soup down gratefully. The priest made his way to my bedside. His face was as wrinkled as an old apple and his scowl only made it worse.

"The sisters have told me how you came to be here. God was watching out for you that day, I'm sure," he said as his gaze drifted down to my bandaged hands.

Having him stand by my bedside reminded me of the musty-smelling priest of the small church my mother had forced the family to attend during my childhood. I had never taken to the whole Catholic thing, but I also didn't want to offend my hosts, so I just nodded.

"How are you feeling, Mr. Ainsworth?" Helena asked, her smile steady and unwavering.

"Good, excellent," I said, praying Father Griffith wouldn't peek under my bed. "My head is definitely feeling clearer."

"Let's see how your head is healing." The nun leaned forward, her small fingers delicately peeling off the square of gauze taped to my left temple.

"Where are you from, John?" the Father asked, walking to the window across from my bed.

"Burford, Father."

"That's Oxfordshire, isn't it?"

Helena folded the gauze and placed it on the tray beside her. From a pocket, she pulled out a small glass jar containing a dark, burgundy-coloured substance. When she twisted the lid off, the smell hit my nose instantly—a vinegary, acrid scent.

"I've been meaning to ask, Sister, how long have I been out?" I flinched as she dabbed the tincture onto my head.

"The sisters told me you were brought here three days ago," Father Griffith replied.

Helena smiled, pulling clean gauze from the tray. My scalp tingled, grew numb, and the faint ache that throbbed beneath the skin faded.

She wrapped my head up again and began the process with my left hand.

"Are you able to call someone, one of my friends? Let someone know where I am?" I said to her, watching her unwrap my hand, curious to see the damage.

"The convent has no electricity and thus no phone," the priest said, observing Helena's tender ministrations. "I am sure, however, that one of the nuns can let a villager know and have them call your friend."

When Sister Helena pulled the final piece of cloth away, I was relieved to see the damage wasn't as bad as I was expecting. My joints were aching, but the cuts had shut completely and were covered in thin, brown scabs. Helena applied the tincture and wrapped my hand back up again.

"Are you the—" I paused to find an appropriate word. "The leader of this...?"

"No, no, not at all. I manage a parish closer to London," Father Griffith said, smoothing out his cassock. "I'm visiting on business as it were, along with a deacon who is mentoring with me."

"Sister Agatha May will be coming by shortly," Helena said softly, her eyes still downturned. "We'll get you out into the fresh air for a bit before dinner."

"Well, John, I will see you for dinner then," the priest said and took his leave, his hands still clasped behind his back.

I heard him greet someone in the hall, then another nun entered, pushing an old wooden wheelchair. This nun, who must be Sister Agatha May, was also dressed all in black with her curly brown hair loose, hanging down past her shoulders like ribbons. She pushed the chair right against my bedside, arranging it so it would be easy for me to slide in.

"It's a pleasure to meet you, Mr. Ainsworth," she said, her voice high and seeming on the verge of laughter. "Your chariot has arrived."

"It may not look state-of-the-art, but it was the best we could do. We borrowed it from Mrs. Walsh in town," Helena said.

"No, this is great. Thank you. I appreciate you going to such efforts to make me comfortable," I replied.

"Don't worry, we'll be gentle with you," Agatha said, tossing back the blankets and hooking her hands beneath my calves.

She pulled me to the edge of the bed and then braced a foot against the wheelchair to keep it pinned against the side of the bed. Helena slipped her hands under my arms and lifted me over the edge of the bed and into the chair.

Between them, I could smell something. A sweet, clinging scent like roses. The tips of Helena's soft hair brushed against my face for a brief moment, as tender as fingertips. Then I was seated with my bandaged, useless hands resting in my lap.

The chair rolled forward as Helena pushed me away from my bed and out of the room into a low hall. I was more than a little curious to see the rest of the convent, the rest of the nuns.

The hall immediately outside my room ran the length of the building and was open at one end where evening-softened sunshine crept in. Even from where I sat, I could smell the heady scents of sunbaked grass and pollen-heavy flowers. At the end closest to my room was a large wooden door—the front door of the building itself.

Helena pointed to the set of double doors across from us. "Our sanctuary. As a guest here, please refrain from entering that room. It's a private place."

I jerked back against the chair a bit as Helena guided me over the stone floor down towards the sunlight. The hall was lit by a single small window to the right of the door at one end and the open entryway at the other. A thin wind, still hot from the summer's heat, whistled through the length of it.

We passed a few doors, all closed, and a set of stone stairs that led up to a second floor. Each wooden door had its own mosaic of water stains and age spots. As we went, Helena pointed to one or another, telling me where it led. A doorless threshold for the dining hall, the following door for the kitchen. Across from it, the closed door to the room where Father Griffith and another clergyman were staying. Apparently, my room was most often used for a medical ward. The last door led down to the cellar.

She told me all this without prompting, as if there were no secrets in the Crimoria Convent.

Ahead of me, Agatha's black habit fluttered like wisps of smoke as she led the way down the hall and out into the open air, into the light. Transitioning from the naturally cool hall into the wall of heat, still unabated by the fading of the day into evening, was a shock to say the least.

The wheelchair rolled smoothly onto the stunted grass and then stopped. Sister Agatha May spun on her heel—indeed her heel, for I saw when the edge of her habit lifted, that she was barefoot—and gestured out around her with a smile on her face.

To her left rose delicate vines tied to tall trellises. Other nuns, bare-headed and bare footed all, walked among the plants. I twisted in my seat so that I could look up, over my shoulder, at the convent itself. The simple building was tall, two storeys, structured from weathered stones and topped with a peaked, gray-shingled roof. The low sun glinted off the few windows that still contained glass, while the ones without looked more like the empty eye sockets of a dusty old skull.

The building was in shabby shape, and it looked like part of the rear wall had collapsed and been repaired with red brick, which stood out drastically next to the original gray stone. Off to the right and left of the building were piles of stony rubble, sweeping off the sides like wings.

"Our home used to be much larger, Mr. Ainsworth." Helena's soft voice in my ear made me flinch a bit.

Agatha laughed at my reaction and kneeled in front of me, picking up my hands gently in hers.

"What happened here?" I asked.

"In World War II, the enemy mistook the convent for a military base in the night," Agatha said softly. "We lost forty of our sisters that night and the majority of the building itself."

"That's—that's awful. I'm sorry."

Agatha stood.

"Old wounds heal and the scars remain to remind us," she said. "It's important to remember and appreciate each and every day."

I waited for her to continue. Instead, Helena pushed the chair forward across the grass, bringing me closer to the field of vines. Agatha stepped up to the vine nearest and rubbed a leaf between her thumb and forefinger.

"Are those grapes?" I asked.

"They've been struggling this summer with the drought," Agatha replied.

"We make wine, a small enough batch every year, but it's enough for our needs," Helena added.

"I knew monks sometimes make beer, but I guess I never knew that nuns made wine as well."

Helena pushed me onward, past the length of the humble vineyard. Beyond it lay more rubble, the remains of the back of the convent. It looked like the original structure had been quite large and the green space I was in now would have been an inner courtyard. Along the border of these stones, which defined the shape of the building that had been, was a small patch of dirt where sprouting plants struggled. Two nuns stood among these dying vegetables with watering cans.

My eyes stung as sweat ran down my forehead and I tried to wipe my face on my shoulder. The sun sank below the treeline, the sky faded from a hazy yellow to a washed-out gray, but still the heat was overwhelming. I had just made up my mind to ask Helena to wheel me back to the shelter of the convent when Agatha spoke up again.

"We nearly starved that winter, but by the charity of the villagers, we made it through."

"Didn't the Church help? Didn't they send anyone? Anything?" I asked.

Helena wheeled me around to face the convent again, where the thirsty grapevines wilted in the heat. A couple of nuns walked through the trellises, touching a leaf here, testing the dirt there. As I watched, two more nuns appeared from over a hill, both carrying buckets, which they brought to the vineyard.

Standing guard at the end of the vineyard, a scarecrow hung from a wooden frame, arms outstretched, dressed in dark rags with a wide brim hat on top of whatever wrinkled, dried out vegetable that served as its face. Then I was rolling again. The heat was so intense even the scarecrow seemed to be wilting.

"The summer after that winter was harder still," Helena said. "We had no stores, our cellar was buried beneath the rubble, and the villagers had to look after themselves. We were all starving."

The nuns in the vineyard straightened up, pressing their hands to the small of their backs, stretching, and watching as I passed.

"What happened?" I was surprised at my own interest. I almost felt invested in the convent, in the survival of these nuns from more than thirty years ago.

"The Mother Superior died," Helena said.

"Our revered Mother Sabine Celeste," interjected Agatha, walking at my side, her hand on my shoulder and face upturned to the sky.

The open-ended convent beckoned with its dim coolness.

"She made the ultimate sacrifice and the convent lived on," Helena finished, just as I was enveloped by the darkness inside the building.

The wheels of my chair trembled on the uneven stone floor as I was guided to the archway that led to the dining hall. As I was brought in, I could see that this long room was lit with weak evening light coming in through narrow, glassless windows and a few gas lanterns set upon a long, age-darkened, wooden side cabinet. The cabinet's doors were gone, revealing shelves laden with plates, cups, trays of cutlery. Behind the cabinet, between two of the windows, was a doorway that had been bricked up. It must have led to one of the old wings of the convent, before the bombing destroyed it. The plain table was framed on its two long sides by simple wooden benches. Helena positioned me right at the head of the table, as though I was a guest of honour.

I sat there and watched the nuns work, setting the table with the chipped plates, tarnished silverware, and wooden cups from the side cabinet. The women ranged in age, in hairstyle, in complexion, but they all seemed happy as they worked. Their movements were easy, practiced. They did this every day and I wondered if they ever got bored or annoyed. I tried to imagine these serene women bickering but couldn't.

They set the table and I watched the nuns, all dressed in shabby habits faded to cloudy black with frequent washings and careful patching.

None wore the typical head coverings I was familiar with. Their hair hung freely in different lengths, different colours, but all free of the typical wimples I was used to seeing nuns wear. There were six in the room with me, including Sister Helena Rose and Sister Agatha May. Seven more joined, carrying platters of food, setting them carefully onto the table. Then, as one unit, in a strange, graceful unison, the nuns sat down all along the benches.

They waited, heads bowed, eyes closed, their rough and reddened hands clasped in front of their chests. The smell of the food finally hit my nose and my mouth began to water. The food smelled plain, lightly spiced, but fresh.

I wondered if I should pray as well or just wait it out.

The sounds of heavy footsteps echoed down the hall, growing louder and louder, until Father Griffith appeared in the wide door followed by a younger man. The younger man was probably around my age, dressed in similar clothes to Father Griffith but looking a lot less stern. His clean-shaven face was pale and his cheeks were covered in a light spray of freckles. He trailed after the priest like a shadow, clutching a rosary, running its beads through his fingers.

Griffith's hands were behind his back and he surveyed the silent nuns, the set table, and frowned. He looked at me, his frown deepened. Slowly, the priest paced down the length of the table to the opposite end and something there made his frown transform into a scowl.

He sat on what must have been a low stool waiting at that end of the table. I heard the wood squeak under his weight, and he shifted, trying to get comfortable. The height of the stool must have been low indeed because the edge of the table was level to his chest. To my right, I thought I saw Agatha's lips curl up with the hint of a smile. The young man followed and sat down on another stool next to Father Griffith's, just as low as the first.

The priest cleared his throat, a wet and thick sound that reverberated through the stone dining hall in a thoroughly unpleasant manner. With that unnerving introduction, he began his prayer.

"Bless us, O Lord, and these, Thy gifts, which we are about to receive from Thy bounty. Through Christ, our Lord. Amen." He crossed himself and the other man did so as well.

I waited for the nuns to repeat 'amen.' Instead, they opened their eyes and immediately began serving the food. Agatha took my plate from in front of me and filled it before her own. Griffith watched them, his mouth gaping and hands clenched on the edge of the table.

Neither of the nuns sitting closest to him took his plate or filled his glass. It was like he wasn't even there. His companion looked at him, then at the nuns, finally at his empty plate. The young man stood, the stool clattering behind him, and picked up their two plates.

He fumbled with the dishes, trying to reach through the seated nuns to a platter of potatoes. The plates teetered precariously and one slipped, clattering to the table.

"Sister Angelica, would you assist the deacon? He seems to be struggling," Agatha said, a laugh beneath her words.

A nun nodded, taking the plate from the deacon. His face went red and he stammered an apology. She carefully made up the two plates and handed them back to the deacon, who hastily returned to his seat.

Griffith's eyes met mine over the long table as the young man placed the plate down in front of him and I had an idea that I should say something, thank him for his prayer or something. I opened my mouth, then felt a soft touch on the top of my right wrist, just above the edge of the gauze.

Agatha held a cup up to me, her head bent a bit so she looked up at me through her eyelashes.

"Our very own vintage from 1967," she said.

She didn't wait for my response, instead pressing the lip of the cup against my mouth. The scent of the wine struck me first, like heady perfume—intimate and overwhelming. Then Agatha tilted the cup and I tasted the wine for the very first time.

It was like nothing I had ever tasted before, nothing I could ever forget. While its scent was delicate and teasing, the taste was powerful and sensual. It slipped into my mouth like the tongue of a lover, tasting of rich decadence and dark pleasures.

I shivered as I swallowed.

My face felt hot and I prayed I wasn't blushing.

"What do you think?" Helena asked, reaching over to cut my potatoes.

"It's—It's amazing." My inadequate reply.

Agatha stood, going to the side table to retrieve a bottle, and returning with it. She held it out to me, label up. The label depicted a detailed drawing of the convent under a crescent moon. Beneath the drawing of that familiar structure, in cursive, were the words: 'A Special Red Wine Lovingly Produced by The Sisters of the Crimson Vine.'

"Beautiful, isn't it? Our own Sister Bernadette Marie drew that," Agatha said. "Mr. Olliver in town prints the labels for us himself."

I wasn't able to reply as Helena popped a bite into my mouth. Down the table, Father Griffith cleared his throat again.

"I should think that John would be able to manage supper on his own," he said, loud enough to be heard over the talking nuns.

Helena, ever serene, didn't look his way.

"Mr. Ainsworth's hands are still bandaged. It's imperative that he rest them for a full recovery," she said and I received another slice of chicken to chew.

It was a mix of flattery and embarrassment to be fed like a child by two doting women, by two strangers. Helena didn't allow me a chance to speak. Every time I swallowed, she was there with another morsel, or Agatha had the cup up for me to sip from.

The wine was burgundy sparks every time it hit my tongue, making my scalp tingle. And every taste of it was something new, a hint of something more. Every swallow elicited the same shiver, not one of chills but of pleasure.

Before I knew it, my plate was clean and my cup was empty.

"More?" Helena picked up my plate.

Her plate was untouched.

"No, no thank you. I'm stuffed!" I said, loathe to make her spend any more time on me.

She smiled and settled back, picking up her fork and knife.

"You'll have more wine, of course, Mr. Ainsworth," Agatha commanded, her tone at once flirtatious and firm.

I couldn't help but wonder if she was one of those girls who had chosen to be a nun or had been sent by her parents to get her away from a man—or men—until they were ready to marry her off. I shook my head mentally. That was an ugly thought. An unfair assumption towards a young woman just trying to be friendly.

Plus, surely that was an archaic practice and nuns nowadays were all voluntary members of the clergy. Regardless, my cup was full, and I didn't resist when she brought it to my lips again.

I had never been much of a wine drinker, beer and gin being more my style, but this wine was quickly converting me. My own dinner taken care of, Agatha and Helena focussed on eating theirs. Across the table, Father Griffith picked at his food, still scowling at the nuns around him.

"The wine, it's the best I've ever tasted," I said and wondered at my flustered state.

"It's what keeps us fed and warm in the winter," Helena said, picking up her own cup and looking deep into it as though it were a scrying glass.

I wondered what the crimson depths were showing her.

"Year after year, the grapes are nourished in the soil that our sisters died on. Their blood fed the earth and, in turn, the earth feeds us," Agatha said.

As one, the nuns raised their glasses high above their bare heads and intoned:

"Blessed be."

They drank long. I watched their throats as they swallowed and, when they put their cups down, their lips were stained scarlet. Across from me, at the other end of the table, I saw that Father Griffith's scowl had gotten even deeper, etching furrows into his face. Neither he nor his companion had poured themselves any of the wine.

Another sip and I was pleasantly numb, sunk back in my wheelchair with ease, eyelids heavy. The soft conversations of the women around me were soothing, like the whisper of a river.

"Mr. Ainsworth, we've kept you up too long," Helena said.

I tried to rouse myself, but my protestations were ignored.

"I'll take you to bed." Agatha stood, as did the priest.

"I will take John back to his room. I'm sure you're needed here to help clean up after dinner," he said, nodding to his companion who followed the priest as he made his way around the table.

His rudeness shocked me awake. I sat up straighter, and looked to Agatha for her reaction. She only smiled, sat back down, her hands resting on her lap. Father Griffith's footsteps echoed on the stone floor. Hearing them so clearly was what made me realize how quiet it had become in the dining hall.

Each nun sat, hands clasped in lap, watching the priest make his way behind me, roughly jerking my chair around, and pushing me from the room. All the while, the young deacon shadowed the priest, fidgeting with his rosary. My last glimpse of the nuns was of their smiles, small and patient as they watched us, the men, leave.

The ride back to my ward was short but unpleasant. Behind me, the priest grumbled under his breath, and I could tell that he was displeased about something but prayed he would spare me the awkward conversation of hearing why.

Once he navigated the narrow doorway, he positioned the chair next to my bed.

"Up you get," he said, hooking his hands under my armpits.

I tried not to cry out as he roughly dragged me from the chair onto the bed in painful jerks. At one point, I began to slide off the side of the bed and had to catch myself with my broken leg, nearly biting my tongue clear in half from the pain of it while the young man stood in the doorway, awkwardly, uselessly. Eventually, I was situated, though the pleasant buzz of the wine was gone.

Even worse was when Griffith sat on the edge of my bed, his arms crossed. It was then that I knew he meant to air his grievances to me now. He shook his head, clearing his throat.

"Truth be told, John, it's a relief to have another man here," he started. "Father O'Halloran here is helpful, of course, but these past three days have been difficult. These nuns are rather set in their deviant ways. Maybe you could help me, as a fellow Catholic."

I don't bother to correct him on his assumption of my religious practices.

"Deviant?" I said instead.

"I'm sure you've noticed. Going around without shoes, with their heads bare and immodest, their lack of prayer and devotion. They don't even hold mass!"

He stood, his agitation clear, and began to pace back and forth alongside my bed in a rather distracting manner. O'Halloran slipped further into the room and looked at an empty bed for a few moments before sitting and placing his hands in his lap, fiddling with his rosary again. I closed my eyes, hoping the priest would think me exhausted and leave.

"I've never seen one reading from the Bible or carrying rosaries, or even a crucifix of our Lord on the walls," he continued. "And imbibing at dinner as you saw? I'm afraid they've strayed off the path. Yes, I'm sure they are in need of guidance, of intervention from the Church. O'Halloran agrees."

The deacon nodded when the priest looked at him.

"Oh?" I said, wishing they would leave.

Griffith sucked on his teeth, staring at the wall above my bed as if hoping a crucifix would just suddenly appear. Through the open door, I heard the clatter of dishes as the nuns cleaned up dinner.

"I'm sure you've been wanting to ask me my purpose here," said the priest. "Your curiosity is, of course, natural, and I am happy to explain."

I leaned my head back against the wall and gave him a strained smile, lips pressed so hard together that they ached. I thought of the wine, of the nice buzz I'd had. My leg throbbed and I wanted nothing more than to sleep.

"You see, I was honoured enough to be tasked with reviewing the state of Carmel of the Immaculate Heart of Mary."

"I—" I stopped.

"Yes, my son?" he asked, placing a warm, damp hand on my forearm.

"I thought this was the Crimoria Convent? That's what Sister Helena Rose said," I finished and immediately regretted it when I saw Griffith's expression.

On the bed next to mine, the deacon shook his head slowly with a frown.

"That's not the real name of the convent," O'Halloran said. "Not the name the church gave it."

I was surprised at how deep the young man's voice was. I had imagined his voice to be meek, quiet, soft, not as booming as it was.

"These nuns have been rather troublesome." Griffith thankfully removed his hand at this point to clutch the wooden cross that hung in front of his cassock instead. "They have been making wine and passing on none of the profits to the Church. It's a shame to see how far this house of God has fallen."

"They told me that they didn't sell the wine." I found myself feeling defensive for the women here, for Helena and Agatha. "They only traded it to the town for things."

Griffith just sighed and shook his head. "They dedicated their lives to God and as such should provide the fruits of their labour to the Church."

"Did the Church abandon the convent after it was bombed in World War II?" I asked.

O'Halloran's mouth gaped and he looked at me then at Griffith. The priest stood and straightened his shoulders back, looking at a spot just above my head instead of at me.

"I'm not sure where you got that idea from, John." He shook his head. "Frankly, it's a wretched thought. The war was a hard time for everyone, including the Church, and all had to make do with what they had. Now, if you'll excuse me."

He stood over me, made the sign of the cross, kissing his fingertips and brushing them across my forehead to finish before leaving the room. His human shadow followed, closing the door. Finally alone, I slumped against my pillow, sinking down. My hands and leg ached ferociously, and I wished I had another glass of that astounding wine to take the edge away from the pain.

Instead, the pain pricked at me, keeping sleep at bay. I stared up at the ceiling, arms at my sides, suffering in the heat. I counted sheep. I tried to imagine myself at a beach somewhere. I replayed scenes from the most recent film I'd watched.

At some point, I must have dozed off because I woke some time later, when night had fully eaten away all light in my room except a faint streak of moonlight over the stone floor. I felt tense and searched for what had woken me. Around me, the convent was silent.

Then I heard something faint. I strained to identify it. It sounded almost like someone retching. I could hear soft voices, but not what they were saying. The retching continued, a pitiful, unnerving sound.

"Hello?" I called.

The voices faded. I waited to hear barefooted steps coming my way. The retching continued, but as I waited for someone to come, I fell asleep again.

Part II

Crushing

I woke from a dream of being held by a woman dressed completely in red. Her skin, the silk of her clothes, blended together in seductive softness. Her face was obscured in shadow, a crown of grape vines entwined with her golden hair. I rose from her maternal embrace reluctantly, returning to my new lodgings in the convent.

Lying in my bed, bathed in that special golden light of an early summer morning, I enjoyed my own sense of stillness. The whole convent seemed paused on the edge of an expectant breath, waiting for the day to develop far enough to pop the spell cast over the building.

A faint footstep brought me out of my lethargic daydream of the woman in red half remembered. I heard Sister Helena's laughter ring through the hall, bouncing off the grim stones towards me. The door to my ward opened and there were Helena and Agatha, bringing their cheer in with them.

"Let's see those hands, Mr. Ainsworth," Helena said, ever the tender nurse.

Her attention on my bandages made me suddenly aware of how my hands felt. The aches I'd had only yesterday, just before bed, were gone.

"Perhaps it was providence that brought you here now," Agatha said, stripping the sheets from me and placing clean, folded clothes on the bed by my knee.

"Why's that?" I asked, half listening, half concentrating on the mesmerizing way Helena unwrapped the gauze.

"The anniversary is approaching and this year it is more important than ever."

"The anniversary?" I looked up at Agatha's young, gleeful face. "Of what?"

Agatha smiled and picked up a shirt, shaking it out. Based on its general wear, it was likely a donation from one of the simple farmers that lived nearby.

"The anniversary of our Mother's sacrifice. We call it Sabine's Solstice," she said.

"Well, Mr. Ainsworth, looks like you've healed up nicely." Helena set the stained bandages on the bed.

I was expecting red welts at best, thick angry scabs at worst, but instead there were the barest pink marks on my palms to indicate where I'd cut them to ribbons on my windshield.

"Holy shit," I breathed and then felt myself blush. "Oh jeez, sorry, sisters!"

Helena smiled and tapped a pale finger against one of my miraculously healed palms. "Your leg should be following along shortly. Maybe a day or two more."

"Two days? For my leg? I thought you said it was broken!"

"Didn't Father Griffith tell you?" Agatha said with a wink. "God works miracles."

I stared down at my hands, clenching and unclenching my fingers. I remembered the crash. It wasn't a clear memory, rather it was jumbled images laced with phantom pain. But I remembered cutting my palms deeply as I climbed through the windshield. I remembered the blood slicking my skin and running down my wrists. Red drops on the grass like wet rubies.

I clenched my fists again and forced a smile as I looked up at the nuns.

"Get ready," Agatha said, patting the pile of clothes.

The two women gave me privacy by waiting out in the hall. I pushed away the nagging thoughts, the memory of blood on grass, and the flesh that had hung from my palms like strips of raw bacon.

I pushed the thoughts away because pain could distort memory, stretch it out, exaggerate it. I knew, for sure, I'd hit my head during the crash. Chances were I'd misremembered the severity of my injuries.

Right now, with all my senses, I looked down at my hands and saw them healed. That was the truth. It just couldn't have been as bad as I'd remembered.

Feeling more centered, I pulled off the yellowing sweat-stained shirt I wore, leaving it crumpled on the bed. The loose pants I wore, the left leg cut short just above the knee and the top of the cast, would have to stay. Knowing the nuns would be waiting for me out in the hall, I wiped my body with the damp cloth that had been left and pulled on the clean shirt. Hefting my cast, I slid off the edge of the bed into the wheelchair and wheeled myself to the door. It felt great to be able to use my hands, to have power over my own travel, but Helena wouldn't hear of letting me wheel myself to the dining hall, instead postulating that I still needed to go easy on my hands.

She pushed me past the dining hall, to the very end of the building, and out into the growing heat of the day. Despite the early hour, the other nuns were all hard at work in the garden and among the trellises. Bees buzzed loudly over the dying grass, descending in lethargic spirals to rest on wilting dog-rose blossoms. Helena situated me so my back was against the rising sun, facing the vineyard.

After making sure the wheels of my chair were set just so, she sat down on the grass beside me, watching the toils of her sisters. Her blond hair, now back and braided with a bright green ribbon, caught the sunlight like fire and reflected it brilliantly, giving me a brief illusion that her head was surrounded by a halo.

I turned back to my view of the vineyard where the nuns examined the leaves and vines, as they knelt in the dirt pulling weeds, or tipped over buckets of water onto the soil. The dark scarecrow loomed over them, arms outstretched as though to swoop on them like a hungry crow. It was hard not to look at it, not to stare.

"Who made the scarecrow? It's rather macabre." I tore my eyes away from the thing and looked down at Helena's upturned face.

"We all made it. All of us, together," she said with her signature enigmatic smile. "Last summer."

"It must be pretty sturdy then, to have survived the winter." I refused to look at it.

A bowl was thrust into my view, and I took it out of reflex, then looked up. Agatha handed another bowl to Helena, then sat down on my other side with her own.

"Sister Angelica's famous porridge," she said, throwing her head back as if to drink up the sunlight.

"I think the word you're looking for is 'infamous,' Sister Agatha," Helena said.

I took a bite out of curiosity and pushed the gluey sludge around my mouth before reluctantly swallowing. It slid like cement, oozing past my esophagus, and settling in my belly with a weight I knew I would regret later.

"This helps," Agatha offered up a cup and I took it, swallowing back some before realizing she'd given me wine.

That rush, again, like a relentless tide pulsing through my body. I sighed, letting my hand holding the bowl sink down to my lap. Helena plucked the cup from my other hand and sipped from it.

I watched as her eyelids drifted shut, her throat working as she swallowed. I wondered if she felt the same sensations I did drinking the wine, or if it was something else entirely for her.

A nun among the vines stood, stretched, and looked over. The bottom of her habit had been pulled between her legs, tied to a simple rope she wore tied around her waist, which transformed the habit into something similar to a pair of coveralls. Picking her way through the rows, she stepped out onto the yard. The nun was short, barely standing at 155 centimeters, and her lined face framed dark blue eyes. Her hair was salt and pepper, straight as a razor, hanging to her waist. When she stood in front of me, she untied her habit from her rope belt, letting it fall to her feet again.

"Mr. Ainsworth, this is Sister Bernadette. She's the one who manages the bottling part of our winery," Helena said and Bernadette grabbed her habit again, this time to give a curtsy before sitting down in front of me.

"I'm surprised you'd punish our guest so." Bernadette nodded to the bowl in my hand.

"Oh no, really, I quite like it."

"You shouldn't lie to a nun, Mr. Ainsworth. Haven't you heard how capable we are with rulers?" Agatha brought her hand up in a fist, as though about to slap a ruler over my wrist.

"Hush, Agatha!" Helena scolded with a smile.

I couldn't help but laugh despite how strange this behaviour seemed for nuns. Of course, I was no expert. all I had to go off was my experience in a strict Catholic school when I was younger.

"How do you think your vineyard will do this year? The crop, or whatever it is you call grapes," I said.

"Tis been a harsh start, but after Sabine's Solstice, the grapes will come back stronger than ever," Bernadette replied.

"The last report I caught from the weatherman was that they expected the drought to last the full summer." I stared up at the unforgiving sky, void of clouds.

Bernadette stood, placing her hands on the small of her back, and stretched backwards. Straightening up again, she leaned over me, placing one dirt-dusted hand on my cheek.

"Have faith, Mr. Ainsworth," she said, then she returned to her vines.

Agatha plucked my bowl from my lap, gracious enough not to comment on its fullness, then retrieved Helena's.

"I'll take these to the kitchen." And she disappeared back into the convent.

Helena and I sat in silence, watching the nuns work. The heat was growing by the minute, and I could feel sweat trickling down the back of my neck and into my shirt. I couldn't say I had much faith in the survival of their grapes.

"I'm surprised we haven't seen Father Griffith up and about," I said, mainly to distract myself from my growing discomfort.

"He is on the second floor, in the office," Helena replied. "Cataloguing our records and making a report for the Church. Unfortunately, Father O'Halloran fell ill during the night and is having a lie-in."

I thought back on the dinner of last night, of Griffith's generally sour attitude, and didn't feel like I was going to miss his company that day. O'Halloran, though, had seemed a decent enough person. Guilt—familiar guilt drilled into me by my religious mother and the strict nuns who'd taught me at school—raised its weasely little head. I heard my mother's shrill voice echoing in my mind: "It's common courtesy! Don't you want to be a good boy?"

"Maybe I should visit the deacon," I heard myself saying. "Check in and see if he needs anything from me."

"As you wish." Helena stood, and I immediately regretted my offer.

She wheeled me out of the sunshine, back into the relative cool of the convent. Evidently, the priest and deacon were put up in a room just a few doors down from me. Helena knocked on the door and when we had an answer, she opened it, and I was brought inside.

O'Halloran was standing next to the window, dressed.

"Father, you must be feeling better," Helena said.

He turned. Even from across the room, I could see he was pale and sweaty. The room reeked of vomit and feces. Unlike the ward I was stationed in, the church visitors had been afforded a smaller chamber with only two beds. One bed was made, the other was not, the sheets stained with something I didn't want to examine further.

"Father, is there anything I can help you with?" I forced myself to ask. "I know I can only do so much, considering my state right now."

O'Halloran tried to straighten up, then pressed a trembling hand against his belly with a grimace, his lips twisting.

"Something I ate, I suppose. The sisters have been tending to me as graciously as they can," he said.

Helena went to the bed and gathered up the soiled bed linens, stripping the mattress without a single hesitation as to what her hands might be coming in contact with. I repressed my wince of disgust, lest the deacon see it.

"I'll bring some clean sheets for you," she said and, regrettably, left me alone with him.

He leaned against the windowsill, as though life itself were hanging from his shoulders, adding together all the sins of those he knew to his burden. He looked older than yesterday. He seemed weary.

"Father Griffith says that God gives each of us a job, a calling," he said, sighing—a mix of pleasure, of regret.

I looked over the room, feeling awkward and ill at ease. It was as plain as mine. No crucifixes, no tapestries, no paintings. Just white-washed walls, peeling ceiling, and simple wooden furniture.

"Despite my discomfort, I will prevail. As God wills."

"Yes, I'm sure," I replied.

I felt bad. I'd come here to help, possibly comfort, but I hated being here, having to tolerate the awkward conversation.

"Father Griffith has assigned me to audit the convent's records. See their profits and where they have gone." The man coughed into his hand, a wet, horrible sound. "Normally, profits should partially go to the Church. This convent hasn't contributed in decades, despite the winery."

I thought of what Sister Helena and Sister Agatha had told me, about their suffering, about the Church abandoning them in World War II. I couldn't feel much sympathy for the Church's pockets.

"It's a shame," he continued, mopping his glistening forehead with a handkerchief. "A shame that they might not be fulfilling their God-given duties to the Church. No matter. Father Griffith will get to the heart of the matter and help them find the path again. He specializes in that kind of thing, you know. The Church sends him if they suspect a flock has gone astray."

Helena returned with fresh sheets and began making the bed.

"Sister, I believe I am recovered enough to resume my work. Mr. Ainsworth, would you please join us? I think the Father would appreciate it very much," the deacon said.

Helena turned and looked at me, then at O'Halloran.

"The office where the records are kept is on our second floor," she replied, gesturing a hand towards me.

"You have crutches, surely."

The nun and the man looked at each other. I wondered if O'Halloran noticed her hands slowly clenching into fists.

"Of course, Father. If Mr. Ainsworth feels comfortable with climbing the stairs, I'd be happy to bring him some crutches."

She looked at me, her characteristic gentle smile back on her face. I cleared my throat.

"Mr. Ainsworth," the deacon pleaded. "I would greatly appreciate your assistance and since you are staying here recovering, I am sure you are looking for something to help pass the time since there are no Bibles readily at hand for your studies."

I was trapped so I nodded. A few moments later, Helena had returned with some worn crutches. O'Halloran leaned against the window, wiping his forehead, and looking washed out and faded. Helena held the crutches in one hand and used the other one to steady me. I got out of the wheelchair and relished the stretch and pop of my limbs as I stood. Settling all my weight onto my good leg, I took the crutches from Helena, tucking them beneath my armpits.

"Excellent, follow me." The deacon went past us, still slightly hunched.

"Take care on the stairs. Some of the steps are worn slippery," Helena said.

"Thanks for these," I replied and reluctantly followed the man out into the hall.

I didn't have to worry about falling behind as O'Halloran mounted the stone steps with painfully slow progress. I stayed a few steps below him, planting the ends of my crutches firmly before hopping up to the next stair.

The staircase was lit solely by the sunshine that lay like solid ribbons across the stones from the thin glassless windows. The relative cool air of the first floor didn't make it to the second floor with us and I was sweating when I finally reached the landing.

On the second floor, all the doors here were open, revealing small, plainly furnished bedrooms. As I passed them, I caught snippets of the personalities of those who lived in each one. Here was one with fresh flowers in a small vase on the bedside, another with several sketches taped to the stone walls. The next had piles of books on the floor, and yet another with a basket of knitting. Simple rooms, filled with care and life, made as comfortable as possible considering.

The deacon shuffled down the right, leading us to the very end of the hall to the only closed door. Knocking, he leaned against the wall, wiping at his forehead, and waited. Father Griffith opened the door a moment later and greeted the two of us with a grimace, before returning deeper in the room. O'Halloran and I followed him inside.

Larger than the bedrooms we'd passed, this room was brilliant with fierce sunlight. There was a large, well-used desk covered in papers and accompanied by a few chairs at one end of the room. Behind the desk were three short bookcases filled with ledgers, files, and books. The other end of the room had a small table with four chairs. Two windows flooded the room with light. Hanging on the wall were the only pieces of art I had seen in the convent—besides the sketches in one of the bedrooms.

Each piece was a talented rendering done in pencil, framed in rough wood. One caught my eye immediately because it was familiar. It was a detailed drawing of the front of the convent, the very same one that the nuns used on their wine labels.

The piece of art next to that one was of the vineyard and of the scarecrow standing guard off to the right of it. Or at least, this must have been another scarecrow because the one in the drawing was dressed differently and wore an old fashioned wide brimmed hat. A sharp halo had been drawn over its head in black, like a crown of barbed wire.

Next was a depiction of the vineyard again, its vines heavy with grapes. Nuns kneeled around its perimeter, bare heads bowed in deep prayer. This was the only drawing with colour. The grapes were a brownish-red colour, some flaking in places.

The largest of the drawings was a painstakingly detailed portrait of an old nun. Unlike the ones I'd met here, this nun still wore the traditional wimple and held a rosary in her clasped hands. She had been drawn in a three-quarter profile, her eyes uplifted, her expression soft and divine. A lot of love had gone into this drawing.

I heard Father Griffith settle into the chair behind the desk with a soft sigh. The wood squeaked under his weight. O'Halloran collapsed into one of the chairs at the table, clutching the edge of the table so tightly his knuckles went white. I made my way over to the desk and settled in one of the plain chairs at the front, setting the crutches against the wall next to me.

A clatter of dishes heralded the appearance of a nun at the office door. She was a young woman, perhaps just beyond early twenties, with closely cropped blond hair—a surprisingly modern hairstyle. She slipped in holding a tray laden with a teapot, two cups, and even a plate of simple biscuits. This tray she deposited on the table in front of the ailing deacon, pouring some tea in a cup and setting it in front of him.

"Thank you, Sister Angelica," Father Griffith said as she placed a steaming cup in front of him.

"Of course, Father. Enjoy," replied the nun. "My apologies, Mr. Ainsworth. I didn't realize you were up here or else I would have brought you a cup. I can go back and retrieve one if you'd like."

"Don't worry about me, Sister. I'm fine," I replied and she nodded, disappearing back out into the dim hall.

"The nuns have, thankfully, kept meticulous records of their work," Griffith said after waiting for Sister Angelica to be out of earshot and twisting in the chair to pull a ledger from one of the bookcases.

He offered it over to me and I took it. The cover of the ledger was faded to the point that it was hard to read the text on the front, which indicated that these records were from 1965. The priest pulled out the ledger that had been next to mine, setting it on the cluttered desktop and opening it.

"What should I be looking for?" Just asking the question made me feel like I was his accomplice and I regretted it.

The priest opened one of the desk drawers and pulled out a small pad of foolscap along with a couple pens. He slid it across the desk, so it rested between both of us. There were already notes scribbled down the length of the yellow page and he tapped it with a finger. At the table, O'Halloran cradled his head in both his hands, panting a bit.

"Mark down how many bottles they made and what they traded it for, especially if they were paid for the wine." Griffith paged through his book until he reached the first line of records. "The sisters have told me that they only trade the wine for supplies that they need, however, I have found several entries where passing visitors have paid for these bottles. Such profits should have been shared with the Church."

I opened my ledger and stared down at the faded ink on the page in front of me. Flipping through, I could see that each page was carefully filled with dates and entries on what the nuns received for their wine, and what they spent money on. I settled on a page and saw that they had traded three bottles to have their roof repaired after a freak hailstorm.

Going to the next page revealed that a passing family had stayed the night and bought a bottle to take with them for twenty pounds. I stared at the entry. Whichever nun responsible for that entry had added a small note beneath the purchase: "lovely family—little girl asked to try on a habit, found her a spare—precious thing spent the day in it, helping Sister Bernadette in the vineyard."

The priest coughed wetly, audibly dislodging something in his throat then swallowing it back again. I closed my eyes against the assault against my eardrums and took a deep breath before opening my eyes again. The priest pulled the notepad to him and scribbled something down, gathering his evidence against the sisters to punish them for using whatever small profits they made off their wine to keep their convent standing, to keep themselves fed. I flipped the page without making note of that transaction.

I spent the next stifling hour skimming over the record for 1965. Each day was a diary of how simply these nuns lived their lives, dealing with each difficulty as it came and frequently helping out the village and any stranger passing through. They used their wine to buy manure for their garden, to buy medicine when nearly half the village was stricken by the flu, to buy milk and eggs from local farmers.

Occasionally the narrative was broken up by the record keeper sharing her thoughts or marking down a special event: "Mrs. Boswell safely delivered her first baby girl, has decided to call the child Joanne, has the sweetest blue eyes." "Brought a bottle to Mr. Brown who is still struggling to recover from bruised ribs he sustained from falling off his horse." "Great harvest this year, Sister Beth is particularly proud of her crop of potatoes, some of which are as large as two clenched fists." Little moments of their lives captured in footnotes by the diligent bookkeeper.

Father Griffith shook his head, clicking his tongue. He stabbed a finger against the ledger in front of him and looked up at me. "Right here, someone paid over two hundred pounds for six bottles of wine and not one pence was sent to the Church. So disappointing."

He made another entry on the growing list.

"These records are from years ago and it looks like they used the money for upkeep. Does it really matter if they didn't send some of the profits to the Church? It doesn't really look like they're turning a huge profit or anything," I said, shutting my ledger and pushing it away from me.

The priest looked from my closed ledger and back to me with a frown. "I'm sure I must seem like some kind of bad guy, targeting these women. But they dedicated their lives to God and have been failing in following through with their vows. What may seem like bullying is guidance. I was sent here to guide the women and bring them back to the path so that they can reap the rewards given to all faithful Christians."

He ruined his own righteous speech by slouching a bit against the edge of the desk, clearing his throat thickly.

Feeling stiff, I pushed myself up onto my feet and stretched. I hopped around the desk and began browsing the books on the shelves. It was a library with an eclectic range of topics and were most likely donations from travelers or the villagers. There were books on history, travel, and art. Other volumes included biographies, a French dictionary, and a few mysteries. But no Bible anywhere.

I pulled out one of the mysteries, obviously well-loved since the spine was heavily cracked and the pages inside showed where corners had been folded down to mark people's places. I tucked the book into my waistband and collected my crutches.

"I'm feeling a little worn down. I think I'll head downstairs and take a nap," I said.

"Of course," the priest replied, not looking up. "You are still on the road to recovery. Go on downstairs and I'll see you at lunch."

O'Halloran raised his head as I left, silent, his face as pale as curdled milk.

Going down the stairs was definitely more difficult than climbing them and it was hard not to imagine how many bones I'd break if I slipped. Finally at the bottom, I could feel every tense muscle in my body relax. I thought about going back outside to see if Helena or Agatha were out there, to talk, but decided to go back to my room instead. Having to deal with the sour Father Griffith had drained me of every bit of energy I'd woken up with and I didn't want to worry the sisters if they thought something was wrong.

Kicking open the door to my room, I closed it behind me for some privacy, then made my way to the side of my bed. Someone had placed a pitcher of water on the side table, along with two cups—one empty, one with wine. My armpits felt bruised from the old crutches and it was nice to sink down into the bed and take the pressure off. I pulled the book from my waistband and opened it to page one, helping myself to a sip of the wine while I was at it.

Lost in a vague daze—a result of the heat and the wine—reading and re-reading the passage where the protagonist is locked in a mysterious cellar room, I was roused by a soft knock on my door and struggled to sit up. Helena entered, the wheelchair rattling in front of her. I rubbed my face with my hands, trying to shake off the clinging drowsiness. The oppressive heat in the room weighed on me and I felt completely out of sorts, lost in a hot, wet swamp.

"You must be starving, Mr. Ainsworth. I came to collect you for lunch but thought you must be dozing, so I couldn't bear to disturb you," she said, smiling as she tapped a finger on the cover of the book lying open on my chest.

"Oh, uh, I borrowed this from the office, I hope that's not a problem," I started.

"Not a problem at all." She picked it up, placing the novel on the table next to my bed. "This one is an excellent choice. The twist at the end is very unexpected."

"What time is it?" I still felt fuzzy, but from the quality of the light, I knew it must be getting late.

"Six o'clock. I came to get you for dinner. Do you want to use the crutches or the wheelchair?"

My armpits were still aching, but I didn't want Helena to have to push me again, so I grabbed my crutches and, together, we made our way to the dining room. The air was slightly cooler, though I wished I'd had a chance to clean up a bit before dinner because I could feel the thick coating of sweat that lay across my skin.

The nuns were busy setting out plates, glasses, platters of food, and bottles of wine. Helena directed me to the head of the table again, where there was a stool waiting for me. Agatha was already sitting to one side and Helena took the other side as I lowered myself down, propping the crutches against the wall behind me. Unlike the stools given to the clergymen, this one was the right height for eating. It was hard not to feel a little flattered at how my treatment differed from that of the priest and deacon.

Across from me, at the far end of the table, was Father O'Halloran looking worse for the wear. He was trembling as he kept his handkerchief pressed to his forehead, eyes cast down at the table in front of him. Next to him was the ever-scowling Father Griffith, arms crossed as he watched the women work.

As the nuns sat and began to serve themselves, the men didn't seem to notice or desire to offer a prayer. Sister Angelica placed two full plates in front of the men, and Father Griffith picked up his fork, mechanically eating small bites. I wondered if Angelica had been assigned the duty of showing the two men hospitality or if she was big-hearted enough to have volunteered to help the sour old man. Either way, she delivered their food with a smile, even when Father Griffith snapped at her to take the wine away and give them water instead.

"Father O'Halloran still looks under the weather," I whispered to Agatha.

The nun looked down the table at the deacon with a small smile.

"I'm afraid our humble food has not agreed with him," she replied and filled my cup.

I forgot all about poor Father O'Halloran as soon as the smell of that wine hit my nose. I embarrassed myself a bit as I gulped down half before I was able to slow down, feeling the rush over my body as the alcohol hit my belly. Was this how alcoholism started?

I forced myself to set the cup down and take a slow, deep inhale. Agatha and Helena were on either side of me, watching me with bemused gazes. I felt my face heat up and tried to think of something to say to distract them from my obvious embarrassment.

"You said you celebrate the death of your former Mother Superior?" I said. "What kind of things do you do?"

"It's my favourite day of the year," Agatha said. "All the villagers join us here at the convent."

"Usually, we start by sharing a meal out by the vineyard," Helena added. "The villagers bring food, we provide the wine. We eat together, then as night falls, we offer up some prayers."

"The best part of the night is when we put up the new Guardian," Agatha said, resting her chin on one hand as she stared off in the distance.

"Guardian?"

"The scarecrow we keep by the vineyard," Helena replied.

"It's a beautiful ceremony, a ritual we've done every year to honour the Mother Superior," Agatha said.

"What kind of ceremony?"

"It's hard to explain, you'll just have to see it for yourself," Helena said, refilling my glass.

Across the table, the deacon groaned a bit, clutching at his stomach. Father Griffith stood, hovering over him, helping him stand. Together, the two left the dining hall, and I didn't envy what the deacon was going to experience in the toilet next.

I finished my dinner, happily washing down every bite with more and more wine until I had achieved a pleasant buzz. The nuns began to clean up, leaving behind the bottle of wine nearest me. Agatha and Helena stayed seated, keeping me company and my cup full. Eventually, it was just the three of us sitting in the empty dining hall.

"So, this ceremony, it's to promote your harvest? I didn't know Christians did that kind of thing," I said.

Helena smiled, refilling my cup.

"Father Griffith said that he thought you all had strayed from God's path." I bit down on my tongue as soon as I had said it, mortified.

I felt the pause that hung in the air as if it were a heavy weight across my shoulders, crushing me. Then Agatha laughed, a bright sound that sliced through the hot air. A deliberate laugh, almost cruel.

"Well, we can't exactly argue that. However, there are many ways to worship, Mr. Ainsworth, and we are still very much religious," she said.

"So, you still believe in God?"

"We believe in something greater than ourselves, something powerful, something that watches over us and protects us," Helena answered without answering.

"Do you believe in God, Mr. Ainsworth?" Agatha asked, a playful tone in her voice.

I laughed awkwardly.

"I'm not sure, honestly," I said. "I was brought up Catholic, but it's hard to believe in something you've never seen."

"We agree on that point then, Mr. Ainsworth," Agatha said and tapped her cup against mine.

"I also have a hard time believing in an all-knowing being that would punish a good person just because that person didn't specifically worship it." I knew I was rambling now, I usually avoided religion as a conversation topic. "Why would a God be so egotistical? To allow a murderer into paradise because he believed in God but send someone else who has only ever tried to do their best in the world to hell? What kind of God is that?"

"Not a kind God, to be sure," Helena murmured and she poured me the rest of the wine.

I woke up, rising through tendrils of clinging sleep. Moonlight fell softly across the empty beds like ghostly whispers. A weak wind whistled against the windows, rustling the trees I could see through the glass. I pushed myself up to a seated position, rubbing my face and feeling overheated. I thought of the conversation at dinner and groaned. What must the nuns think of me? Getting drunk and then rambling on about God and religion.

"I'm such an ass," I said, staring up at the ceiling.

Just outside my door, something scraped against the stone. A chill rolled down my spine as I froze in my bed, my fists still pressed against my forehead. It was an irregular sound.

Scrape, scrape, pause. Scrape, long pause.

In the otherwise silent convent, the sound was as loud as screams and sent goosebumps all over my body.

The low moan that accompanied the scraping made my shiver deepen. Caught in the grip of a growing foreboding and yet, unable to resist my own curiosity, I got out of bed, balancing on my good foot. I hopped over to the door, trying to be silent, and pressed my ear against the wood.

Accompanying the scraping was a low, desperate moan punctuated by panting. All these sounds created a sickly cacophony. The dirge of a dying beast trying to find a safe place to leave behind its mortal prison. A dark corner in which to die. I put my hand on the knob and paused. It might be better to just go back to bed, hide under the covers like I had when I was a little boy. But like in a bad dream, I couldn't resist opening the door just a crack.

Just past my door, crawling his way towards the entrance, was Father O'Halloran. He was dressed in a threadbare, old-fashioned nightshirt and his whole body was convulsing. He had one arm stretched out, fingers digging into the grout between the stones, pulling himself along. A man-sized slug. He looked up as I opened the door and stared down at him.

"Help me," he whimpered.

I went down onto my good knee, stretching the plaster-bound leg out to the side.

"What are you doing?" I whispered. "Do you need me to take you back to your room?"

I reached out to him and he gripped my hand in his. I could feel how cold and clammy his skin was, and I wanted to pull away in revulsion.

"The food," he gasped. "The food!"

"Yes, Father, I heard that you got food poisoning. How about I get you back to your room and get you some water?"

As I said that, I remembered my leg and tried to think of how I would even be able to help at all. I leaned out farther, looking up and down the hall, hoping a nun might be taking a night-time walk or patrol, or prayer, whatever it is nuns might do at night. I thought about going upstairs and knocking on a door to get someone to help but realized that I didn't even know which room might be Agatha's or Helena's. Then I thought of Father Griffith. Of course. He was on this same floor and would be able to carry Father O'Halloran back to bed.

The deacon jerked my hand, pulling me down towards him. I could smell his breath, tinged with the thick aftermath of vomit.

"You must take me elsewhere, take me out of here, to the village or..."

His whole body shook so hard he dropped my hand, curling in on himself, his head tapping against the stone floor.

I gripped the door frame, pulling myself up. "I'm going to get someone to help."

He moaned, a sad wheedling noise, then tried to reach for me again.

"Agatha?" I called, my voice echoing through the night-shrouded hall. "Father Griffith?"

"No, no, no," the deacon panted.

"Anyone?" I reached for my crutches.

The man retched, his whole body heaving, and his back humping up as he vomited onto the floor. A thin, watery pool of black bile funneled between the stones, vile smelling rivers.

"Oh dear." A shivery voice, full of amusement.

I looked up and saw a nun walking towards us. She wasn't one that I had formally met and I was at a loss for her name, but she was stunningly beautiful. Her thick, red hair hung down in heavy curls to her waist, unbraided or tamed in anyway. Her pale skin was spectral in the darkness, seeming to float since her black habit was almost invisible in the shadows. She looked tall, towering over us as she approached.

Then she deigned to sink to our level, kneeling and pressing a hand to the back of Father O'Halloran's neck. She looked up at me. Her eyes were dark, endless, and I could feel myself falling into them.

"He's running a fever," she said, breaking her enchantment over me.

The deacon whimpered as she rolled him over, not very gently at that, treating him like he was a sack of grain to be inventoried rather than a suffering human being.

"I thought it was food poisoning," I said, looking down at O'Halloran's panic-stricken face.

"It's the stomach flu, poor man."

He was still reaching for my hand, though now his eyes were closed, and he was whimpering his way through a frenzied prayer.

"Maybe we should take him to a hospital," I said, staring down at him with pity.

"Of course. I'll be sending someone to the village immediately, but until then, he is in good hands. Just like you," the nun said and her smile gleamed in the darkness.

She slipped an arm around the deacon and stood, pulling his limp body up with her like he was a doll. I stared up at her, shocked at the surprising strength she had just shown. She made her way back down the hall, taking Father O'Halloran with her, his feet dragging along the floor.

I watched her take him into his room and then his door shut. I stayed there, listening. The warm night wind whistled through the hall, rushing in from the open end that led to the vineyard.

It was a long time before I left my threshold vigil, wincing at my cramping leg, and hopped back to bed.

PART III

Fermentation

"A nun with red hair?" Helena paused her inspection of my cast.

"She came to help with Father O'Halloran last night."

I was lying in bed, feeling exhausted from tossing and turning all night, the mystery book I'd borrowed lying open on my chest. Agatha was sitting on the windowsill across from my bed, staring out across the woods and fields.

"That would be Sister Philippa," Helena said after a moment.

"I can see Mr. Thorogood coming up with his wagon," Agatha added from her perch.

"Is he coming to get Father O'Halloran?"

"Father O'Halloran has already been taken care of. Mr. Thorogood is here to help with preparations," Agatha replied.

"Your leg seems to be healing nicely. I think we'll be able to take this cast off tomorrow." Helena smiled, straightening up and smoothing out the front of her habit.

"That—" I struggled to pull my thoughts into some kind of order. "You said it was broken."

"Yes, I did," the ever-serene nun said.

"It can't be healed." I said. "Broken legs take weeks of healing not—not days!"

"We will see more when we remove the cast, of course," she replied.

No matter what these nuns said, I knew they had to be wrong. They weren't doctors, just nuns. Maybe they had helped tend to old people or childbirth, but they were mistaken. If my leg was already mended, as they claimed, then it was never broken. Maybe cut up or severely bruised, maybe even just a slight fracture. But not broken.

"We take good care of our guests here." Agatha joined Helena at the side of my bed and tapped the spine of the book, which lay still on my chest. "Are you at the end yet? I always thought it was silly how the protagonist acts, fainting at any sort of inconvenience."

Pushing away from jumbled thoughts, I looked down at the well-loved paperback novel. It lay open at the three-quarter mark.

"I'll bet you won't be able to guess the killer's identity." Agatha laughed and let her hand rest on the cast that covered my leg.

"Hush, Agatha, don't tease him so," Helena adjusted my collar, smoothed out the fabric. "Mr. Ainsworth, will you be joining us outside for breakfast?"

My mind, unbidden, plunged backward, into the night and onto the terrified face of the deacon as the nun—Sister Philippa—picked him up and pulled him back down the hall like a blood-thirsty specter in the night. In that moment, I felt my skin rise in goosebumps as I wondered if I truly had a choice here or if I was just as much at Sister Helena's mercy as Father O'Halloran had been at Sister Philippa's. I looked up at her serene face, her soft eyes gazing over me, her pale hands clasped in front of her. I wondered if I would care if I had no choice.

"That'd be lovely," I said.

My leg was itching horribly, and I dug my nails into the skin around the top of my cast, powerless against the sensation. Luckily, for me, breakfast was eggs and bacon rather than Sister Angelica's infamous porridge and distracted me from the itching.

Still, I stared down at my plate and heard the echo of Father O'Halloran's pleading voice: "The food! The food!" My stomach growled in response, and I decided it was worth the risk, digging in while people bustled about all around me. I watched men from the village as they set up benches and long, rough tables, while the nuns tended to the grapevines. Just at the edge of my viewpoint, I could see three nuns digging a hole in the ground.

"Is that part of the celebration? Is it a fire pit?" I asked.

Helena and Agatha followed my gaze to the three nuns digging, digging, digging.

"It's a grave."

I whipped my head to stare at Agatha. She looked back at me from where she sat on the grass next to me. She was smiling. A chill sunk into my heart.

"It's for the scarecrow, Mr. Ainsworth," Helena added, laughing behind a delicate hand.

I looked at the three toiling nuns and then over at where the scarecrow hung from its pole, looming over the vineyard still.

"You're going to bury the scarecrow?"

"The act of burying the old scarecrow represents the death of the old season, of our bad luck. We will erect a new one to represent a new beginning, of our rebirth. It's to symbolize a new start, a sacrifice for a new beginning," Helena replied.

"Oh." The longer I stared at it, the creepier the thing looked. "I guess that makes sense."

In the background, I could hear the shovels striking dirt, hear the dirt thudding against the ground as it was thrown from the hole. The nuns worked unceasing, untiring. Over the sound of their shovelling was the laughter of the villagers as they worked, the whispers of the nuns among the vines or in the garden.

As the heat rose, my vision of them wavered as the air around them shimmered. Their forms, the vines, the hills, and villagers all danced, their shapes shifting, becoming a strange living mosaic made of flesh and heat and movement.

I swallowed and heard that too. Everything felt amplified, intense. My head buzzed. I could feel the sweat trickling down the back of my neck, down my sides. The scarecrow seemed to wave its arms at me, to come alive, struggling against the rope that bound it to its stake. The air slid into my lungs thick as syrup, my leg itched and itched and itched.

"I think I should head inside. The heat is—it's a bit much." I struggled with my crutches, got to my feet.

"Leave your plate, I'll handle it," Helena said, taking it without waiting.

She and Agatha watched me go. I could feel their gazes on my back, as hot and unrelenting as the summer sun.

It was a relief to escape into the convent, where it was, at least, slightly cooler. I stood in the shade of the hall, gasping, trying to identify the source of my disconcertion. Even there, I could hear those shovels and it gave me the shivers.

I hopped farther down into the hall, standing in front of the room where Father Griffith was staying, thinking to ask after his ill companion. I wrinkled my nose. I could smell something sour, something rotting. I couldn't hear anything. I touched the tips of my right index and middle fingers against the doorknob, the metal cold and blackened with age.

I turned the knob, froze.

I tried to process what I was seeing. Still balancing the crutches under my arms, I pulled my hand from the doorknob and spread my fingers to see the palm better. The scabs were gone, replaced by faint, thin scars. Scars that looked years old rather than the result of wounds from an accident a few days ago.

I clenched my hand into a fist with no hint or whisper of the old pain. Beyond the door, came soft prayers. Father Griffith. His prayers summoned that good old Catholic guilt and I knocked. The prayers stopped and I listened to the approaching footsteps. The door opened and a wave of stinking sickness rolled over me. I pressed the back of my left hand against my mouth and swallowed back a gag.

Father Griffith looked exhausted, pale, with heavy bags under his eyes. He held a pocket-sized Bible in one hand and gripped the door frame in the other as if it were the only thing holding him up.

"Father Griffith? I just wanted to check on you. I heard Father O'Halloran was taken to a hospital?"

He shook his head, turning away from me and going to sit on a bare wooden chair that had been placed near the window. "They took him last night. In the middle of the night. Witching hour."

"Father O'Halloran seemed rather worse for the wear, so it was probably a good idea that he was taken to a doctor, right?"

"A doctor." Griffith echoed, shaking his head.

I wavered on the room's threshold, neither entering nor leaving. "I'm sure he'll be right as rain in a day. I guess the nuns didn't have the right supplies to help him?"

"They won't take me to see him," Griffith said. "They claim they can't find someone to take me."

"They seem busy with the event—"

"There's something wrong here. These nuns, these *women*, they can't be trusted." The priest stood, slapping his Bible against an open palm.

"You can't be suggesting—" More than ever I regretted knocking on the door.

"God will protect me, son." He held up the Bible. "And God has his eyes on these women and a reckoning will come upon their heads. I won't stand for any of this! Any of it!"

Griffith's face was red, glistening with sweat as he held his Bible up towards the ceiling, as if waiting for his god to do something. His voice boomed against the stone walls and I leaned out to look down the hall to see if any of the nuns were near, if anyone else could hear the Father's rantings.

"And you, John. You, a good God-fearing man, you will help me. Together, we will bring justice to this forsaken convent." His eyes bulged and spittle sprayed from his lips like a sun shower.

I took a step back, out into the hall.

"Let me ask, maybe... maybe I can get you a ride or find out where Father O'Halloran was taken." I grabbed the doorknob. "I'll be back in a bit."

Shutting the door, I stumbled back. The back of my shirt was soaked and I felt shaky. For a moment, I'd been afraid. Afraid of the old priest. The way Griffith had gotten so worked up, how he was convinced that the women here at Crimoria Convent were guilty of...

Of what exactly?

Of hurting O'Halloran?

Down the hall, I could see Helena standing in the sunlight directing two men as they carried a table along the grass. I could go out there now. I could go to her and ask her where O'Halloran was, if it was true that they weren't trying to help Father Griffith.

But even just the thought of asking seemed absurd. Worse, it might make Helena think that I was agreeing with the priest. That I thought she and her sisters were suspect of something. Capable of something. What exactly? Murder?

Instead, I laboured up the stone steps to the second floor. I went slowly, trying to place each crutch down in a way that kept them quiet. Guilt rode me all the way up to the deserted second floor, all the way down the hall to the office.

The back of my neck prickled, I glanced over my shoulder to find the hall empty, the bedroom doors closed. I passed through the sharp shafts of scorching sunlight that lay across the stones, slicing chunks out of the false twilight that filled the hall.

In front of the closed office door, I rested my fingertips on another doorknob, sucked in a breath, and opened the door. The office was empty, the folders and books still where the priest and I left them on the desk. I sat down in the chair behind the desk and flipped through the open ledger, glancing over the figures and transactions.

A decade ago, they traded three bottles of wine for well repairs. After that, they gave a bottle to a villager as a birthday gift. The nuns here truly survived off what they could make with their modest vineyard. I flipped back through the years until I got to the last page. About to close the ledger, I paused.

I went back to the first page, then the last, then picked a place in the middle. I turned, pulled another ledger towards me, checking the first and last pages. I checked a third ledger, then a fourth. I stared down at the lines of data, separated in columns for description, amount of bottles traded or sold, and the name of the person or company who received the wine.

Despite the intimate heat of the stuffy room, I stifled a shiver. I went back to each ledger, checking the first page of each—the title page, in which the year was written in the same careful handwriting that made up the meticulous ledgers. And beneath each year was the sentence: "Recorded faithfully by Sister Angelica of the Crimoria Convent.

I twisted in my seat and reached, pulling several more of the thin ledgers out of their homes within the sagging bookshelf. Each one was populated with the same careful writing, though the ink faded as the years progressed backward in time, changing from black to gray to a mere shadow of words. Sister Angelica's name was on each first page, dating back five years, then ten, then two decades. Piles of ledgers balanced on the desk in front of me, open to their first pages.

"Impossible," I breathed, staring down at the front page for 1946.

I thought about Sister Angelica, pulling her face from my memory of seeing her in this very room only yesterday. She was young, I'd guess twenty-four at the oldest. Not old enough to have recorded these decades of data.

The door to the office swung open and the pages of the open ledgers fluttered in the resultant displaced air, causing me to flinch.

"Mr. Ainsworth, I wondered where you'd gotten to," Sister Helena Rose said.

She stood in the threshold, half her face shrouded in the darkness of the hall, giving her the illusion of having lost half her head. I shuddered. Then she stepped further into the room and the light from the window chased the shadows away. Helena padded to the front of the desk and looked down at the haphazard piles of ledgers. I had the feeling she was deliberately not looking at me as she carefully began to close the ledgers and neaten the piles.

"Father Griffith must be very grateful to you for continuing his work while he is... praying in his room," she said, her tone as soft as the velvet that covered a cat's claws.

I closed the ledger and placed it on one of the piles she had created. I then clasped my hands in my lap so she couldn't see them shaking.

"I don't really think what the Father is doing is all that constructive, considering," I said, carefully, purposefully. "I was really just more curious about what life is like here, I guess."

The nun looked up and smiled. With that small gesture, I felt that moment pass—a moment balanced on a knife edge. Which side had I landed on? Helena began to pick up the ledgers, placing them back on the shelves.

"Our existence is not something the Church enjoys. They've sent many priests over the years," she continued, standing behind me and the hair on the back of my neck rose. "Men who demand entrance to our home, to our records, to our profits."

Her small, pale hand slipped onto my shoulder, and I looked down at her delicate fingers, the nails she kept clipped short. I watched those fingers tense as she squeezed my shoulder once.

"We were left alone to starve. It was through our Mother Superior's sacrifice and the grace of our God that we survived that first winter, that we continued to survive. By what entitlement do these priests feel to come here and seek to command us?" Her voice was right by my ear. "We watched her die. We were helpless, scared, weak. No more. Her death did more than sustain us, it set us free. Free from them."

I clenched my hands tighter as, at the same time, I felt terror grip my heart. Then she was moving back around the desk, turning to the window, her back to me.

"However, life will go on here, as it always does," she said softly, almost more to herself than to me.

I studied her as she stood with her back to me, her entire body lit with gold from the sunlight. She half turned to me, smiling over her shoulder. Gilded like that, she could have been an angel or something else entirely inhuman.

"The Church says those who stray from God's path either go to hell or purgatory." She was so still. Frozen. A thing outside time itself. "But is purgatory so bad, trapped in eternity, free of the grip of a tyrant?"

I was frozen, a mouse in the gaze of a serpent, a mortal in the presence of something revered, until another nun poked her head into the room.

"Sister Helena, the butcher is here and wishes to speak with you about the last order we sent him."

"Of course, I'll speak with him now." Helena made her way across the room, then paused. "Sister Morgan May, Mr. Ainsworth here was just telling me he wanted to learn more about our lives. Won't you take him down to the cellars and give him a tour after lunch?"

Sister Morgan May was taller than Helena, with thick black hair, and bright rosy cheeks which turned an even deeper red as she blushed. She nodded, looking everywhere but me. Helena swept out of the room, taking the magic with her. A moment after, Sister Morgan May made an awkward curtsy, becomingly old-fashioned, then fled.

I stared down at the desk, willed the thundering of my heart to slow. Sister Helena had been her usual, gentle self, but something about the conversation had unsettled me and I couldn't place my finger on what. I listened. Silence. I was alone again, from the sound of it, so I began to open each of the desk drawers.

The middle held the standard collection of pens and pencils, there was even an old black fountain pen and metal pot of ink. The left two drawers held empty ledgers, the same kind that filled the bookshelves. One drawer left, the largest one on the right side, but when I tried it, I found it locked.

I leaned down so my eyes were level with the keyhole. It was the simple kind that most desks had, easily picked with a simple paperclip, which seemed to be the one standard supply missing from this office. I sat back up, turned, and looked at the ledgers. Women took new names when they became nuns—I remembered that from school. Maybe there was a strange tradition at Crimoria, that there was always a sister with the name Angelica, and Sister Angelica always took care of the ledgers.

It was too hot. The office was stifling me, the sunlight reflecting on the bare stone walls and floor, fracturing, baking me. Desperate to leave, I retrieved my crutches, situating them under my arms and standing.

Before leaving, I stopped to look at the pictures hanging on the walls. Specifically, I looked at the serene nun who gazed upward. The very pencil lines that defined her eyes seemed to radiate kindness. I reached out, carefully lifted the drawing off its hook. Turning it over, I saw writing on the back that read: "The Selfless Mother Superior."

I looked at the portrait again, the portrait of the woman these nuns seemed to worship, then I put it back where it belonged and left.

Sister Morgan May's feet were silent on the stone steps that led down into the darkness of the convent's cellar. She darted a look over her shoulder at me and I could see she was blushing again.

"Th-this was really small before, just for—for staples like pickled vegetables and canned fruit," she said. "Watch your head, Mr. Ainsworth."

I ducked beneath a wooden beam and my good foot slipped on the edge of a stair sending me to the dirt floor with a jolt. I hopped, trying to catch my balance, but fell against the rough-hewn wall.

"Are—uh." Morgan took a step towards me, her hands clasped, then flinched away.

"I'm fine! Just fine," I said, laughing a bit, sheepishly. "I'm accident-prone, hence the crutches!"

I balanced on my good foot and, with the crutches beneath my arms, gave her hearty jazz hands. "Tah-dah!" Her hands flew to her mouth, covering a smile and a laugh.

"This way, Mr. Ainsworth, and be careful. Sister Helena Rose would never forgive me if you hurt yourself... again," the nun said and, lighting a lantern, she led me deeper into the cellar.

"You said this used to be smaller?" I asked.

"Yes, it was much smaller and, after the bombing, it had also partially collapsed. When the vineyard grew, we dug it out again and created this space."

The light of her lantern revealed a low room that swept off to the right, filled with wine racks ladened with bottles. Shelves along the stone walls did hold jars of preserves, pickled vegetables, bags of flour, and corn, but the majority of the storage space was occupied by the winemaking tools—barrels, tubing, containers—and the ripe stench of chemicals and aging grapes.

"This is where we separate and clean the grapes, here we extract the juice, here we ferment them."

Now in her groove, the shy sister's free hand fluttered about in front of her as she went on and on about the various tools hanging from the stone walls and stacked on the dirt floor.

"We use this press for crushing the grapes," she continued, laying a hand on what looked like a large wooden barrel with a handle on top.

"But on special days, like the Sabine Solstice, we crush the grapes the old way."

I placed my hand on the top of the wooden presser. It was sticky with old grape skins and stained a deep, deep red along the rim.

The crusher sat on polished metal legs, as tall as my chest, and smelled of a ripe sourness from the old juice.

"The old way?" I asked.

"With our feet," the sister laughed behind a hand.

"Oh!" I said, looking down at her dirty feet, toes deep in the dirt.

She leaned in close, I felt her cool breath waft across my lips, tasting of hints of wine.

"Don't worry, we wash them first, Mr. Ainsworth."

Then she was away, taking her light with her to the far end of the cellar, leaving me to hop after her with a blush on my cheeks.

"After that, we add the yeast—we get that from the village, of course—and ferment the wine for a period of time, about two weeks usually," Sister Morgan May continued. "We use clay from the nearby river to collect unwanted particles, then transfer it all to those barrels to age."

We passed ceiling-high barrels mounted on rusted iron legs, then she stopped in front of the back wall made of large hewn stones weeping moisture. It seemed older than the rest of the cellar. There was a patch in the left side of the wall were the stones seemed dry and the mortar bright, fresh, between them. The new mortar defined a hole that had been thin and tall, nearly as tall as I was. It looked like a new repair job. I could even smell the mortar in the air still. On the ground in the corner was a bucket and trowel, as well as a bag of unmixed mortar.

"This is part of the original crypt. The rest caved in soon after the bombing due to structural damage. We'll never be able to access it again," Morgan said, pressing a hand against the new-looking stones.

"The sisters who died during the bombing were interred in the village cemetery."

"Do you think you'll ever make the effort to excavate it?" I asked and placed my hand on the wall next to hers.

The mortar still felt wet. I wondered what had prompted them to need to replace the old stone. More of the structural damage? I shivered and jerked my hand off the stone, wiping my fingers on my pants. I stepped back, putting distance between me and the wall. The wall that separated us from the dead.

A beat of silence and I watched the nun's shoulders, her back. She was motionless, almost preternaturally still. Then she finally took a breath and broke the illusion.

"No," Morgan sighed. "That was then, and this is now. The past can be good and sweet to remember, but it must always remain the past, and so these sisters will remain in peace."

The sister turned and I shuddered to see how the lantern cast deep sockets of darkness across her face. She raised it, the illusion was gone, and she looked at me for a moment.

"That concludes our tour," she said, her voice the softest sepulchre whisper.

"What—" I swallowed against the dryness in my throat. "The wine has such an ... intense flavour. What do you do to give it that flavour?"

Sister Morgan May smiled.

"The flavour comes from the grapes, the soil," she said and led me back the way we'd come, up the stairs to the main floor.

The sunlight outside was blinding, the heat overpowering compared to the relatively dim, cool of the cellar. A lot had been done while I got the tour and the yard surrounding the vineyard was crowded with villagers and nuns. Weathered wooden tables with matching bench seating had been set up in an arc around the vineyard, centred on the spot where the scarecrow had been. Against the side of the convent, more tables had been set up for what I could only assume would be for food and drink. Beyond all this, between the courtyard and the convent's well, was a towering pile of wood—the startings of a giant bonfire.

I spotted Sister Helena Rose talking to a broad-shouldered man with salt and pepper hair. By the blood-stained apron he was wearing, he looked to be the village's butcher. Helena said something that made him laugh loudly and wholeheartedly, slapping his ample belly with his hand.

More laughter drew my gaze to the garden where a group of young women were helping some nuns set up a cauldron of water over a small fire. The whole air of the place had the intense excitement and anticipation for the upcoming event. The very air thrummed with it, so much so that I began to feel it too.

I turned to a nun as she passed me, one I hadn't been introduced to yet.

"Excuse me," I said. "Can I help with anything?"

The woman shook her head and smiled.

"You just rest, Mr. Ainsworth. Heal that leg of yours."

She moved past, bringing a small box into the convent. I watched her go, then hobbled my way to the pile of wood. A couple of villagers were there, fiddling with the kindling and structure. They looked up at me as I approached, both men, and one tipped his hat at me.

"It looks like this is going to be quite the celebration," I said.

They glanced at each other, then looked back up at me, easy smiles on their faces.

"It always is," said the man on the right.

"A right proper party," said the man on the left.

They continued to stare up at me as they kneeled and I was struck by their unwavering smiles. It seemed like everyone around here, villagers and nuns alike, were always smiling. Unbidden, a chill ran down my back.

"Ah, well," I said, taking a step back.

They both stood at the same time, tucking their hands into the trouser pockets.

"You and that priest there'll be the guests of honour," said the man on the left.

I nodded, turned, and fled their eerie smiles. Smiles that seemed to be everywhere. Limping across the raked dirt, my leg began to throb from the exertion.

"You must be Mr. Ainsworth," came a voice and a hand upon my arm.

I stumbled, caught my balance, and turned to find the origin of the voice. A short, young woman stood beside me. Her mouse brown hair had been carefully curled and tucked away into a bun. She wore thick-rimmed glasses and a demure brown dress.

"Uh, yes, yes, I am. So strange, everyone seems to know my name," I said and barked out a harsh laugh that frightened me.

Another chill rose through me and I was struck by dizziness, wobbling slightly on my crutches. The woman gave me a perplexed look, dropping her hand from my arm.

"Why wouldn't we? We don't get many visitors here, Mr. Ainsworth. It would be stranger yet if we didn't know your name. News travels fast here," she said and I was relieved when she didn't smile.

"Of course, of course," I said, still uneasy, and I looked past her to where nuns were carrying buckets of water to the convent.

"My name is Jolie Miller. I am the primary school teacher down in the village."

I sucked in a breath to ward against the pain in my leg and offered her a hand, which was regretfully sweaty. She took it in a strong grip, and I was able to see that her ring finger was bare.

"Nice to meet you, Ms. Miller," I said. "The whole village gets involved in this, is that right?"

"That's right. Let's go over to the shade and sit. It must get uncomfortable standing on one leg all the time. And please, call me Jolie," the woman looped her arm through mine and led me to the side of the convent where the building cast a large shadow over the grass.

I slid down the bumpy stone wall thankfully and stretched out my legs.

"Do you know the history of Crimoria Convent?" she asked.

"It was bombed in World War II and the Church left them to starve, right? It was because of the village and then the vineyard that the nuns were able to make it through the winters?"

Jolie nodded. "It was horrific. My grandmother told me about it. Most of the nuns died, some instantly in the blast, others slowly suffocated in the rubble. Still others who succumbed to injuries days after the attack. That first winter was hard for everyone. The village barely had any stores for themselves, let alone the surviving nuns."

"And the government didn't send any aid?" I asked.

"None. When the first winter passed and the war finally ended, no one had any hope left. It seemed certain the nuns would die; the village would follow."

"Then the Mother Superior did something, right? The nuns haven't spelled it out for me, but they made it seem like she did something to save the convent and village," I said.

Jolie looked off across the yard to where the thick vineyard grew tangled and lush.

"Crimoria and the village survived. We both live in a kind of symbiotic relationship. That bomb, when it hit, it changed our fates. We're connected forever."

"What do you mean?" I asked, but she only shrugged and stood, brushing grass from her legs.

"It's time for me to head back. I am in charge of the children during the ceremony. They love it so much, they can get pretty rowdy," Jolie said and began to walk away before I could say more.

More villagers arrived, none seemed to drive despite the heavy boxes of vegetables, jars of preserves, and baked bread they carried. They filed past me, entering the convent where the nuns spirited the food away. I saw Jolie stop and speak with Sister Helena, who glanced my way. Then the teacher moved onwards, down the road and towards the village. Helena slipped through the crowds and into the convent, reappearing moments later with two cups in her hands. She knelt by me and handed me one, filled with that familiar burgundy colour of Crimoria's wine.

"Ms. Miller said you were looking a little pale," she said.

Already my mouth was watering and I felt a tingle low in my belly. I tried to only take a sip but ended up gulping a mouthful instead. I closed my eyes as the first rush hit me, submerging me in sensation, my tongue burning with flavour. I didn't know what to think, how to feel. I felt completely out of control. I couldn't seem to figure out what was going on. I didn't know if I cared. If I should care.

"Better?" the nun and I nodded.

"Tell me, Sister, what did the Mother Superior do? I have heard you all mention a sacrifice, a sacrifice that somehow resulted in the vineyard."

Helena looked out across the yard where the crowds thinned as villagers returned down the road to their homes.

"Tomorrow night," she replied. "During the ceremony, I will tell you the whole story of our Mother Superior."

"But—" I started, she shook her head.

"Tomorrow night, Mr. Ainsworth."

PART IV

Clarification

I woke to a room still shrouded in night and my bandaged leg itching horridly. I reached down, trying to push my fingertips into the cast and failing. Groaning, I flopped back against the pillow and rubbed my palms against my closed eyes, sending sparks across my eyelids. Twisting my leg as much as I could inside the bindings provided no relief. Instead, the itchiness seemed to worsen, as if to mock me.

With a sigh, I sat up, swung one leg over the side of the bed, dragged the cast to follow. Fully awake, the idea of the cooler night air outside, whisking away the sweat on my brow, was irresistible. I hooked my crutches under my arms and stood, making my way to the door of my bedroom. All around me, the convent was quiet and still I hesitated to wrap my hand around the doorknob.

Unbidden, the faces of Griffith and O'Halloran floated up through my thoughts. I hadn't seen Father Griffith the whole of the day, not even at mealtimes. I assumed the nuns were bringing meals to his room. I had to assume because none of them mentioned him at all in the course of any conversation. Like he wasn't worth any thought. Just a nuisance to be ignored.

I opened the door and stepped out into the dark hall, riding a wave of vertigo as I lost my bearing in the absolute blackness.

My eyes adjusted and I saw a line of flickering, orange light that outlined the stones in the floor with hellish threads. I held my breath, straining to hear. Soft voices, chanting, a whispering choir. Standing on the threshold of my room to the hall, I stared at the door across from me, whose frame was highlighted from flickering candlelight within.

The sanctuary.

The doors to the convent's sanctuary had been closed since I arrived and that was the one room—besides the bedrooms—was the one place I knew not to intrude. Then again, I had expected mass to have been held in the morning or evening, but it had never happened.

Now I could see movement—shadows shifting back and forth, breaking the hint of candlelight. I made myself cross the hall. As I approached, the voices got clearer. It sounded like prayer. Standing in front of the sanctuary's door, I listened to the melodic susurrus of the nuns' midnight mass.

I couldn't imagine anything more childish than peeping through a keyhole, but I knelt anyway, awkwardly shoving my injured leg out to the side and out of the way. Hands on the door frame, I leaned in, pressing my face close.

In the limited view allowed by the keyhole, I looked onto a hellish view. Hundreds of candles—short, tall, fat, and thin—perched on the two side tables, lined the floors, ringed the small podium at the opposite end of the room. I could only imagine how stifling and hot it must feel in that room, like a corner of Hell.

There were only three pieces of furniture in the room that I could see, the two side tables burdened with their waxen sentinels and the low wooden altar at the very opposite end.

The stone walls were bare of crucifixes or of tapestries depicting Biblical scenes. The altar was too far to tell if it held a Bible or some other sort of religious paraphernalia, though I thought I could safely assume it wouldn't.

And the nuns... The sisters knelt on the hard stone floor in neat rows, their hands raised, their faces upturned. They were naked, the candlelight casting fiery calico patterns across their skin. The nuns fell forward then rose again, hands stretched to the ceiling as their voices rose and fell with their movements.

Whatever language they were speaking, it wasn't English. And whatever they were worshipping, it wasn't anything orthodox. I became painfully aware of how my uninjured leg throbbed, holding the weight of my body entirely in a painful crouch, so I stood.

Beyond the door, the nuns continued to chant—or sing—as they worshipped something beyond my understanding. A midnight mass before their yearly festival to celebrate the sacrifice of a woman long dead.

I considered going back to bed but thought again of the poor priest, so I turned the way I knew the back of the building to be and spotted a square of lightness, the hint of moonlight beyond this stone hall. I was determined not to make a sound across the floor and placed each crutch carefully, holding my breath at times, listening all the while.

As I crept closer to the end of the convent, I began to hear a sound. Soft at first, then more insistent the further I went. It was impossible to deny what I was hearing.

Weeping.

It was impossible to deny what I knew.

The only people sleeping on the first floor were me and the priest.

I groped blindly in the dark, probing outwards with the ends of my crutches until I felt it tap against stone, then wood—a door. I pressed my ear against the wood. I could hear him. He was weeping, then the crying would pause and I would hear frantic whispering... praying. Then the weeping would resume.

I tapped the door with the tip of my crutch.

"Father Griffith? Are you alright?"

At the sound of my tapping and my voice, the room went silent.

"Father Griffith?"

The door opened and I blinked at the bright light that flickered across my face. When I was able to focus, I saw the nun with long, curly red hair standing in the threshold, holding a tall candle.

"Can I help you, Mr. Ainsworth?" she said, her voice as soft as moth wings.

I leaned towards her, trying to look around the edge of the doorway. I caught a glance of a mound beneath blankets, still and silent on the bed. Then the nun stepped over and blocked my view.

"Sorry... I thought I heard something," I said. "You must be Sister Philippa?"

"That I am."

"Is the Father... Would I be able to sit with him for a while?"

"Unfortunately, the priest is still feeling unwell. Disturbing his sleep won't do his health any good," the nun said, unmoving.

"I heard him crying, Sister Philippa," I replied, straightening my shoulders, and taking a step towards her.

The nun didn't move. As tall as me, she met my gaze with unwavering intensity.

"You misheard."

"I did not."

We stood, a mere half meter from one another, the candle between us like a ward. In the silence between us, I could hear the hissing of the wick as it burned. Sister Philippa seemed content to stand there all night, but my armpits ached for holding my weight on the crutches.

"I am sure he would be more than happy to see me," I said.

"If you'd like, you may wake Sister Helena Rose and ask if this is an appropriate way to act while you are a guest here at Crimoria," the woman said, and a small smile crept over her lips.

A chill ran down my back. My resolved cracked. I backed down in the face of this fearsome guardian.

"No, no. That's alright. I-I'll check in on him tomorrow morning," I mumbled, falling back a step.

"Of course, Mr. Ainsworth. Good night," Sister Philippa murmured, now demure and shy, her face ducked down as she shut the door against me and took her candlelight with her.

Doused now in darkness, I listened intently, but the room beyond was silent. I looked down the hall where I could see a hint of moonlight across the trampled grass beyond the walls of the convent. But going outside didn't tempt me anymore, so I turned and went back to my room, shutting the door firmly behind me, wishing for the first time that it had a lock.

Propping my crutches against the wall, I sunk into bed. It was then that I realized that the itchiness had gone, but still, I could not fall back to sleep.

Helena Rose found me the next morning, sitting against the outer wall of the convent, facing the vineyard. I didn't look up at the sound of her approaching footsteps and the back of my neck prickled at the thought of her bringing up my bizarre confrontation with Sister Philippa last night.

"Mr. Ainsworth, I know you have questions. I know you think we are keeping things from you."

"Are you?"

My heart thundered as she stood next to me and looked out over the vineyard, her hands clasped in front of her.

"Tonight is the festival of Mother Sabine Celeste," she said.

"What's going to happen?" I asked and realized, in a sudden jolt, that I was terrified. Terrified at what was to come.

Helena knelt by me and I looked at her, reluctantly.

"I hope you can understand that we normally don't share anything with outsiders. Can you blame us, Mr. Ainsworth? See how even now the Church hounds us and how we must protect our independence?"

She gestured out, her pale hand like a sparrow on the air. I looked out over the vineyard, which struggled under the sun and the heat. Nuns were already walking back and forth from the well, hauling water to the vines.

"Our Mother Superior died to gift us this and they want to take it for themselves. These the same people who collect tithes, who decorate their altars with gold and gems, and eat the finest food, wear the finest cloth. They hunger for more. Like a spoilt child."

I found myself nodding, lulled by Helena's voice. But the fear was still there. Still simmering.

"Look out, look over the rubble and ruin of what was once a home whole and true. A haven and, at times, a prison for generations of women. Women who came here voluntarily, women who were exiled. This is our home and they abandoned us. We would have died, but we survived, we thrived, and we owe them nothing."

I shivered at the rise in her voice, the fierceness and fire that simmered there, contradictory to her placid exterior.

"When I watched my sisters die that night that hell rained down from the sky, I thought maybe we deserved it. Deserved the pain, the suffering. Because we were sinners. A vile doctrine drilled into us from the same Church that left us to starve."

She knelt next to me, leaned in. I could smell her then—a heady mix of the harsh soap that the nuns must use to wash their clothes, fresh dirt, and faintly, a hint of wine.

"But we weren't the sinners. The Mother Superior told us that. She told us every day that we were worthy, as we starved and ate grass and roots, whatever we could find. She told us not to give in. She loved us and she gave her life for us." Helena wasn't smiling now. I froze in her gaze, like a gazelle caught in the glare of a lioness.

"This isn't the first time they've come. The Church sends them from time to time and these priests come here and they turn up their noses at our lives. They lecture us on our ways and demand access to our records. They come here dressed in new clothes, new shoes, fat with food they take for granted. We owe them *nothing*."

I was trapped in a moment with her, surrounded by the hum and buzz of insects, drowning in the heat, caught by her unwavering gaze. She was waiting for me, waiting for my response. I swallowed. Heard my dry throat click.

"What can I do to help?" I said, hearing my own voice's raspiness.

The moment broke and Sister Helena Rose gave me her smile again, reaching out with her hand and resting it on my knee. I didn't relax. The danger had passed, the tension seeping away, but it lurked on the edges of the next moment. Yet at the same time, I thrilled at her touch. My skin tingled from the base of my neck down over my belly, mimicking how the wine made me feel. Hot flashes followed delicious chills through my body as it responded. I swallowed again.

"Thank you, Mr. Ainsworth. When the time comes, I'll look to you then," she said, her voice rumbling like sparking thunder over my skin.

I spent the morning trying to stay out of the way of the nuns, who prepared the convent for the coming influx of guests and for the sacred ceremony. A half dozen nuns bustled in the convent's large kitchen and I watched them manage copper pots nestled on a massive pot-bellied stove. The heat was practically visible, but the women continued to chop, bake, and cook all the while with nary a complaint or break.

Sister Morgan May directed her fellow nuns in carrying crates upon crates of wine up the creaking, groaning cellar stairs while Sister Agatha May helped unpack them onto one of the tables that stood against the outer convent wall.

"Sister, I feel useless. Can I help with anything?" I finally asked Morgan, watching her carefully turn all the bottles label out.

"With crutches?" the nun eyed me up and down. "We want to serve this wine, not smash it over the stone."

"Ouch," I said, unable to stifle my laugh.

"You're our guest, Mr. Ainsworth, and injured as well. Just relax. You'll need your energy for the festivities tonight," Morgan said.

I pressed my right crutch against my side with my arm and saluted clumsily. The nun laughed and shooed me away, ready to receive yet another box of wine. I hugged the side of the convent, trying to stay out of everyone's way, as I slipped around to the side that faced east—the side where my and the priest's rooms were located.

There were no workers here, no villagers or nuns. The others were in the back. The wilting grass on that side was tangled and nearly knee high, filled with prickly thistles and buzzing gnats. I kicked clumps of dead grass aside as I crept along the wall towards the first window. Dust danced up from the ground, shining golden in the sunlight, chokingly beautiful, catching in my throat and harassing my eyes.

Reaching the window, I glanced around to make sure I was unobserved, then I leaned in, peering through the glass. Beyond was the room which had been given to O'Halloran and Griffith. From the window, I could see a single chair stationed next to the bed closest to the door, as well as a side table with a pitcher and cup.

A huddled figure lay on the bed, head hidden by the pile of blankets covering them, despite the stifling heat. Father Griffith. I thought about knocking on the window, catching his attention.

Then I thought about Sister Helena and turned away instead.

The day passed quickly then, as I sat against the convent wall, in the shadow, dozing in and out as people passed by. Then a hush settled over everything, quieting even the hectic buzzing of the flies and bees. I stirred out of my doze, stretching against the sun-warmed stones of the convent wall. My back ached in a way that hinted at future bruises from leaning against the uneven surface. The air had cooled only slightly, and overhead the once bright blue sky had drained to a deeper cobalt tinged with bruise-purple, and clouds had appeared at the horizon, hovering over the tops of the trees that waited to catch the sinking sun.

The villagers were gone. The sisters were gone. Before me, the open space was set for the party—long wooden tables and benches, a woodpile waiting to be lit, and the small little vineyard filled with dappled shadows. Golden flecks danced over the garden at the very back, fireflies like untethered stars fallen from the endless dark sky above.

Stiff from sleeping against the wall, I got up painfully, clutching at my crutches. Once standing, I stretched, feeling—and hearing—my back pop and crackle. Having slightly reduced the stiffness in my joints, I tucked each crutch under my arms, then made my way into the convent.

It was quiet within but not silent. I heard whispering coming from all directions, like the very stones in the walls were sharing secrets. I cocked my head, listening, trying to make out words. It was a futile attempt. I limped down the hallway and saw that the sanctuary doors were closed. When I pressed my ear against it, I found the source of the whispering. The nuns were having another mass. If that's what you could call it.

Beyond the doors, the whispering faded, and I heard shuffling as the nuns began to move. I hurried back to my room, shutting the door as softly as possible. In the hall, the nuns passed my door, their shoeless feet near silent on the floor, their voices still lowered into conspiratorial whispers. I pressed my ear against the door, aching to hear at least a little of what they were saying.

Three knocks resounded against my door, causing me to stumble back, nearly tripping over my crutches.

"Mr. Ainsworth?"

It took me a second to recognize Sister Helena's voice over the thundering of my own heart.

"Sister Helena!" I sucked in a breath and lowered my voice. "Yes, I—I just woke up!"

"The townspeople will arrive soon. I would like to check your leg, if you please."

I scrambled to get to the small cot, to further buy into my lie that I had just been sleeping rather than snooping on the nuns. Flopping onto the mattress, I winced at its subsequent groan but called out, nonetheless.

"You can come in!"

The door opened slowly. As I watched the gap between the door and frame widen, a chill ran through me, an expectation of something terrifying to enter. But it was just Sister Helena who appeared, of course, and I let out a breath.

"You look flustered, Mr. Ainsworth," she said with a small smile and that's when I knew she knew.

She knew I'd been outside the sanctuary, listening, spying. Yet she didn't seem angry.

In her hands, she held a small black case, which she set upon the bedside table.

"Oh, just... uh," I stuttered.

"Just the heat?" she supplied.

"Yes, that," I said, defeated.

Helena kneeled before me, reaching and cradling my cast in both hands delicately. She looked up at me from under thick lashes and I felt my face grow hotter. I clasped my hands on my lap, suddenly incredibly nervous.

"How does it feel, Mr. Ainsworth?"

My mind raced and I tried to snatch my thoughts into order.

"Uh, what feels...?"

My mouth had gone treacherously dry and I swallowed with a click, looking down at her kneeling at my feet.

"Your leg," she said with another smile, though she dropped her eyes to where my hands still lay clasped, sweating, in my lap.

"Oh, fine. Of course. It feels fine."

She knew. She had to know. I hadn't felt this lost in a woman's presence since secondary school.

"I would like to remove the cast to check its progress, if that is acceptable to you, Mr. Ainsworth."

The way she said my name sent a thrill through every centimeter of me, every single centimeter.

"Oh, is that too soon? I mean the accident was only a few days ago," I replied, focussing as hard as I could on the cast.

Helena just kept smiling, reaching over and grabbing the small case she'd brought with her, setting it on the stone floor beside her. I watched, transfixed, as she undid the ties and opened the case, revealing bright, steel tools glinting in the candlelight.

A small surgical saw, scalpels, and forceps lay in my view, chasing away the thoughts of before. Helena chose the saw first, still cradling my cast in her other hand.

"Please stay as still as possible, Mr. Ainsworth. This is delicate work, and I would hate to cut you."

I nodded and sucked in a breath, holding it, as she placed the tip of the saw at the top of my cast. From there, the heat I'd felt before—independent of the oppressive summer drought— faded as she sliced through my cast as easily as one would slice bread. The saw purred as it ground through the plaster. I watched her, relaxing as she hit the halfway point without nicking me, and I couldn't help but wonder what had brought her to Crimoria, what had made her choose this path.

"Sister Helena," I started then hesitated. Would this be considered a personal question?

She paused, the cast split two thirds of the way, revealing my pale and clammy calf.

"Did I hurt you?"

"No, I... I was honestly just wondering what brought you here? I mean, why did you become a nun?"

After a moment's pause, she continued sawing.

"I didn't choose to become a nun, Mr. Ainsworth. I was sent here when I was thirteen."

The saw went back and forth, back and forth, catching flashes of candlelight as it moved.

"A lot of convents were populated by the... unwanted. Crimoria was a place where families could send their less desirable family members. Out of sight, out of mind."

"I hope you don't mind me asking—"

"Why was I sent here?"

I nodded and then realized she was looking down, away from me, so wouldn't have seen. Yet she continued as though she had.

"My uncle started visiting me in the night. It began from when I was eleven. Do you understand my meaning?" Helena asked, pausing to look up at me.

I nodded and hoped she wouldn't continue, hoped I wouldn't have to hear more, regretting that I had asked anything to force her to recount what must have been a horrific experience.

"When I was thirteen, I became pregnant. Worried how this might damage the family's reputation, my parents sent me here. I miscarried soon after, but my parents never sent for me."

The saw sliced through the last bit of cast. Setting the tool back into the case, Sister Helena ran soft hands up and down my leg.

"I'm so sorry, Sister Helena," I said.

"I've moved on, Mr. Ainsworth. You can't change the past, but you can prevent it from defining you. I chose to embrace my sisterhood here and have flourished, even despite the bombing, despite the famine. I'm free here, and no one could ask for more. It looks like your bone has set nicely. Let's have you test some weight on it."

Gripping either side of the sundered cast, Helena cracked it open further. I stared at my leg. It was pale, the dark hairs matted from sweat, but it looked completely healed. To be more accurate, it looked like it had never been broken in the first place. It was... uncanny. No scarring, no bruising, nothing at all.

"Can you lift your leg out, Mr. Ainsworth? Go slow."

I placed my hands on either side of me, gripping the edges of the bed in tight fists. I anticipated pain, but as I pulled my leg free, I felt nothing but a shadow of tenderness. I placed my foot onto the stone floor and stared at it.

Helena stood, nudging her surgical kit further to the side with a bare foot, and offered me a hand.

"Up you go!" she said.

I took her offered hand and allowed myself to be pulled up, though I leaned heavily on my good leg. The nun watched me, cocking her head to the side with a playful smile as she waited. Slowly, I began to place weight on the leg that should have still been broken, that should have still given off pain. Only when I was standing with my weight distributed evenly across both feet did I accept I was healed, completely healed.

"It couldn't have been broken, not really," I breathed, rolling from heel to toes and back again.

The tenderness was there, but it was just a twinge. Just a faint hint.

"Oh, Mr. Ainsworth, it was a nasty break. Sister Philippa had to help me force the bone back beneath your skin before I could stitch you up," Helena replied.

I bent at the waist, searching for a scar, any hint of stitches.

"That can't be true. There's no way I could have healed that fast. It wasn't broken. It's not possible. It's not." I was shaking. I was afraid.

Why was I so scared all of a sudden? I looked at my hands next, where the gashes had been deep and now nothing remained, not even the scars I'd seen yesterday.

"How did you do this? How did you do this to me?" I looked at the nun, holding out my hands to her as if in supplication.

She obligated, stepping forward and taking my hands in hers. She brought them up, kissing the back of each, then let go, holding my face, gazing at me.

"Do you trust me, Mr. Ainsworth?" she asked.

"Yes," I said and was surprised at the lack of pause, at the certainty I felt.

I did trust her. For all the strangeness I'd seen and experienced, for all the moments of fear, I trusted Sister Helena Rose. I trusted her wholly. In fact, I was beginning to think that I was in love with her. Her hands, warm and dry, soft and delicate, still framed my face. She stepped closer and I could feel the heat of her.

"I trust you," I whispered.

"Then trust me now, trust me during the ceremony, and trust me forevermore. I won't let you be harmed, Mr. Ainsworth. I promise you that," she said, her voice the barest whisper.

"Then tell me, Helena. Tell me what's going on."

I reached up and covered her hands with mine. She pulled back, taking her hands away, leaving me with a feeling of lost warmth, a void, a yearning that left me flushed. Distantly, I could hear a rising tide of voices, music, coming from the convent's backyard.

"You should clean up, Mr. Ainsworth. Join us as soon as you're able. I'll be waiting."

With that, Sister Helena turned, picked up her medical case, and swept out of my room, a slight blush across her cheeks to match my own.

I fell back onto the bed, my body whole, my limbs trembling. I forced myself to take deep breaths to try and settle my thoughts.

I heard the celebrations in the hall leading outside before I saw them. First, it was the steady beating of drums, so loud I could feel them in the soles of my feet. Next, as I approached closer, came the cheerful sounds of fiddles and flutes. My healed leg ached only slightly as I put weight on it and yet, it was healed, despite all logic. Despite all the earthly rules I knew.

I stepped outside the convent and was greeted by a twilit scene of revelry. The bonfire was blazing, gilding the nearby grapevines of the vineyard. The tables were now laden with roasted pigs and chickens, crocks of fresh butter, corn on the cob, baked apples, pies of every kind, baked potatoes, bowls of steamed vegetables, and—of course—bottles of the Crimoria wine.

Several villagers sat on stools by the back garden, playing on the instruments they'd brought from their homes. I even spotted a teenage boy playing spoons upon his knee. In front of them, their fellows took advantage of the cheerful music, dancing and spinning about, clapping their hands to the beat.

Older villagers had already selected their preferred spots at the tables, clutching full cups of wine and tapping their feet to the music with smiles on their weathered faces. In between them all were the children. Dozens of children weaving through the adults, clutching bags of sweets, and filling the air with their high-pitched laughter.

The nuns roamed the crowds, stopping to talk, stopping to refill glasses or help up a fallen, crying child. They looked like dark angels watching over the commoners, shifting with the shadows that grew longer as the night grew darker.

I spotted Father Griffith easily. He was set up in the old wheelchair I had used, at the end of the table closest to the bonfire that blazed so merrily. He was slouched, hands laying limp in his lap, his head resting on one of his shoulders. The fire threw sharp shadows over his face, creating the illusion that it was actually a skull that rested atop his neck rather than a proper head. Somehow, in the day I'd seen him last, he'd gotten ill.

O'Halloran's voice echoed in my memory: "The food! The food!"

I shivered.

A strange guilt laid across my shoulders and, unsettled, I tried to find the root of it. My first thought was that I felt guilty for not going to the priest, checking on him. But the guilt was something else, something more persuasive. I watched the shadows dance across the old priest's face, creating a valley in his cheek one moment, then sharp relief over his left eye.

I watched that play of light and dark, then it clicked. I felt guilty because I didn't care, because I didn't want to go over and check on him. He looked so helpless, so miserable, sitting alone at the end of the table, and I did not care.

Shuddering at my own cruel thoughts, I turned away. Sister Helena stood next to me, having crept up as quiet as a tiger on its prey. In her hands, she held two cups and she held one out to me. I took it. I didn't need to ask what was in it. I could smell the wine already and my mouth watered. I gulped the cup down in two swallows, wiping my mouth with the back of my hand with embarrassment.

"Feeling better?" she asked.

I could only nod. She put her cup to her own lips, tilting her head back, allowing me a view of her delicate neck as she finished off her own wine.

"Then let's dance," she said, taking my cup from me and placing both on a nearby table.

She held out her hand and I took it. Then, together, we swept away into the crowd.

We danced for what seemed like hours, minutes, years, seconds. The fire cast her hair in living gold and lit fires in her dark eyes, a sunrise glow to her cheeks. She outclassed me, leading me as we danced. She was lithe and graceful, never even flinching when I stepped on her bare toes a few times. The only time she let me rest was to refill our cups with wine. I couldn't complain. Dancing with her felt holy, it felt sacred, and I never wanted it to end.

The musicians obliged, only breaking for their own wine refills and some small snacks brought to them by partners or friends. Their faces glistened with sweat and I wondered that their fingers and lips must ache for all the playing.

My forehead ran from sweat, from the exertion, from the heat of the night and the bonfire. Helena slowed finally, then stopped.

"You must excuse my selfishness, Mr. Ainsworth. Here I am, forcing you to dance with me, and you're only just recovered," she said, laughing.

My heart ached instantly with the loss of her body near mine. I tried to scramble for a reason for us to keep dancing, but she was already stepping back.

"I should make the rounds. Why don't you get something to eat?" she said, clasping her hands demurely in front of her.

"Yes, of course," I replied lamely.

The nun melted away into the crowd, leaving me to retreat to the long tables, now cluttered with used plates. I sat at the end of one of the benches, pushing a plate hosting some bones and an apple core, to the side. The table I'd sat at was also occupied by three old men, smoking pipes at the other end, talking in low, grumbling voices.

I found a plate that seemed clean enough and helped myself to some bread and pork. I ate what I took, staring at the bonfire, at the dancing sparks that disappeared among the stars. I wasn't hungry at all. I knew I was only eating because Helena told me to. Because it would please her to look over and see me eating.

After finishing my plate, I downed my glass of wine and refilled it. This wine filled me in a way food couldn't. It felt different. It felt healing. It felt like all I needed. At the same time that the alcohol relaxed me, sending tingles through my muscles, I was restless. So, I took my cup with me and began to wander, hoping to bump back into Helena.

The band was still going strong, accompanied by their faithful dancers. The children had failed first and lay napping under tables on the grass, along the rubble walls, and in their parents' laps. I walked around the edges.

The moon hung directly above the convent courtyard, painting the grass, the vineyard, the garden, and all the people in silver highlights. The heat was finally dissipating, leaving my sweat chilled on my skin. It had to be past midnight at this point and despite its preternatural healing, my leg ached slightly from the dancing, the standing, the walking. The nuns allowed the bonfire to burn down, leaving bright coals wavering in the ashes.

My body was flushed and hot, the wine snaked through my veins like honey, and I was floating as I walked among the strangers of the village, eventually finding myself back in the convent, hoping that maybe Helena was here waiting for me.

I was at least a little drunk, I knew that, and I still finished off my cup as I climbed the stairs to the second floor. The bedroom doors were open, the rooms themselves empty. Someone had cleaned up the office, putting back all the ledgers, returning the pens and paper to their drawers.

Feeling a little unbalanced on my feet, I sat in the desk chair heavily and sucked in a deep breath. My body buzzed. The silence of the room was too much, and I knew I would need to return to the party, but I still reached for the drawer.

The drawer that had been locked before.

The drawer that was open now.

It squeaked a bit as I pulled it open, revealing a thick photo album that had been tucked away inside. I placed it on the desk in front of me and opened it. The pages were filled with black and white photos, a timeline of the Crimoria Convent captured in snapshots.

The first photo was of a group of six women in habits in front of the building when it had been whole. Its wings stretched out on either side, much like the wings on the nuns' wimples.

After that were photos of new nuns arriving, of the women helping tend to the sick, of travelling to attend a Christmas mass in London. Here a few of the nuns delivered a care package to a new mother who held her baby and smiled brightly at the camera.

A large photo, commemorating the convent's tenth anniversary since opening. At least fifty nuns stood in rows in front of the building, their heads covered with wimples, all with shoes. But the faces were familiar. There was Sister Helena Rose and Sister Agatha May next to one another. Sister Morgan May stood off to the side, hands clasped tightly, looking shy even in black and white. Sister Philippa towered behind her, a smug smile on her face. Sister Angelica and Sister Bernadette were there as well. Front and center though, was another face I recognized despite never having met the woman. I recognized her from her portrait on the wall: the Mother Superior Sabine Celeste. Alive. At least at the time the photo was taken.

I touched a fingertip to Helena's face. She looked the same then as she did now. So did the others.

I flipped through the rest of the pages in a rush, searching for an explanation. There were a few more photos of nuns delivering supplies to charities, of helping mothers deliver their babies. Then a jump. A photo of the shattered convent and the surviving thirteen. The thirteen nuns I had come to know in my time at Crimoria.

A photo of the vineyard, of the new garden, of villagers coming to help.

A photo of the nuns praying around the vineyard, their heads and feet bare.

The rest of the album was empty.

I shoved it back into the drawer with shaking hands. It didn't make sense. My eyes had played tricks on me. I'd had too much wine, of course. I fled down the hall, down the stairs, ignoring the soreness in my leg.

In the main hall, looking out at the shadowy figures that still danced and rejoiced, I paused to catch my breath. A sound startled me and I tilted my head, listening. A faint trill of laughter. The laughter turned to a softer giggle, then faded to a whisper. I found myself tiptoeing down the hall towards the sanctuary where a faint flickering light slipped from the doors, left ajar, and painted the stones with golden light.

I had never properly seen inside this strange convent's holy sanctum, a small room usually locked, a place where I'd had caught a glimpse of some bizarre midnight sabbath. As I neared, I slipped close to the wall, one hand on the stones for balance, until I reached the double doors. The leftmost one was unlocked and opened the slightest sliver, which was allowing the light to escape.

I wrapped my fingers around the latch and froze when I heard the faintest of moans coming from inside. I pressed myself against the right door, opened the left just enough that I could look, so I could see the source of the sounds.

Sister Agatha May lay naked across a plain wooden altar at the back of the room, the candlelight gilding her skin and casting golden threads through her black hair. She writhed on the altar before a wall painted with a vibrant mural depicting a woman slitting her wrists to feed hungry, sucking vines while nuns looked on and prayed under a living sky filled with twisting wings and dozens of multi-pupiled eyes. As I watched, frozen, she arched her back with another soft moan, her left hand reaching down and gripping the brown hair of Jolie Miller, village teacher, whose head was between the nun's thighs as she knelt at one end of the altar.

Agatha reared up, a hand flung across her eyes as she cried out in ecstasy, her voice resounding against the stone walls. She fell back limp against the altar, a broad smile on her face as her chest heaved. Jolie stood, placing her hands on the edge of the altar on either side of Agatha's hips as the teacher leaned over the nun. Her hair was still tied neatly back. Her blouse was unbuttoned revealing small breasts and a flat stomach. The bottom half of her face was painted with blood.

Jolie smiled as Sister Agatha sat up, wrapping her legs around the teacher's waist.

"Thank you for communion, Sister," Jolie said, running a tongue along her bottom lip.

"And may the Eternal Child bless you," returned the nun as she drew her lover in for a kiss.

I turned around, stumbling down the hall, choking on the close air of the stifling building until I managed to get outside again. It was dark, the bonfire mere embers, the moon and stars seemed muted by the vast abyss that was the night sky. The music had stopped and a hush had settled over everyone.

The crowd was smaller, the children had been taken home to their beds, the tables were cleared of all but the wine. I went to the nearest one and found a glass, filling it to the brim and gulping it down. The wave of pleasure was immediate, the sensations intense, as the wine had its effect on my body, leaving me gasping and wanting more. I wiped my sweaty brow with the back of my hand and screwed my eyes tightly closed.

I heard footsteps behind me, and I straightened up, turned, hoping to see Sister Helena. Instead, Sister Agatha walked past, winking to me as she did, dressed once more in her modest habit. Jolie followed, her head ducked demurely, her blouse rebuttoned and her face cleaned but for a spot of blood on the right side of her jaw.

Everyone gathered around the end of the vineyard where the scare-crow had hung. I searched the crowd and finally spotted the fair Sister Helena. Setting down my cup, I went to her side, jamming my shaking hands into my pants pockets. She smiled at me briefly as I approached and turned her attention back to the vineyard.

I followed her gaze as an older nun, one I hadn't met yet, took center stage in front of everyone. She was a small woman, tiny really, dressed in the same fraying, faded habits all the sisters of Crimoria wore. Her pure white hair was cropped close to her head, her face was all cheekbones and strong jaw, and her eyes were a stunning blue.

Helena leaned over and whispered in my ear. "That's the oldest of us, Sister Vashti Eve. She will lead the Sabine Solstice."

I caught movement in the corner of my eye, turned, and Sister Morgan was pushing Father Griffith closer. His hands were pressed to his face. He was still, tense. My heart wrenched. The air was heavy with anticipation, and I took a step towards him.

A cold hand clutched my wrist. Sister Helena. Though she had reached for me, her eyes remained forward, her face serene. It didn't matter. I understood. I had chosen my side. Settling back beside her, I kept my gaze away from the priest.

"Blessed be the vineyard that sustains us all," Sister Vashti intoned and the crowd around me shouted 'blessed be' in unison. "Blessed be the Mother Superior and her holy blood that anointed the earth beneath our feet and gave forth the saintly grapes of Crimoria. Blessed be her grace that soothed the skies and brought rain in time of drought!"

Beneath my feet, I felt the earth shiver. No one seemed to notice or react, but a chill crept down my back.

"Born of her desire to protect and provide, the vineyard feeds us. It heals us. It binds us together under the loving eyes of Mother," Vashti continued, raising her eyes and hands to the heavens.

"Blessed be!" cried the others, following suit.

"Each year we must remember the sacrifice. We must remember our allegiance. Not to those who abandoned us. Not to those who left us to starve. But to the Mother and her Eternal Child: the grapes of Crimoria!"

"Blessed be!"

"Let the blood sustain us!"

I stumbled as I was pushed forward, pressed on every side by the surging crowd. Sister Helena kept a hand on my arm, steadying me, keeping us together.

"Blessed be!"

"And let blood sustain her!"

The ground thrummed in a familiar rhythm, beating like a giant heart. I could smell the vineyard—rich earth, sticky leaves, and something else.

"Blessed be!"

Silence. I clutched Helena's arm like I would drown without her. Everyone around me stood, hands raised, eyes closed. Many were muttering near-silent prayers, their lips moving like worms on their faces. The ground continued to shudder and the air was electric with pulsing intent.

Sister Vashti lowered her arms and the others copied her with soft sighs. The old woman nodded to Sister Morgan, who pushed the priest across the grass. Once Father Griffith was situated next to Sister Vashti, Morgan bowed her head and retreated back into the crowd.

"Each year, blood must be given back in penitence. Blood for the harvest. Blood for the rain. Blood for the Mother!" The old woman's voice thundered in the still air.

"Blessed be! Blessed be the Mother!" came the reply.

"We were further blessed this year, for we were given strangers so we might not cull from our own flock," Vashti said, reaching down and lovingly caressing the back of the priest's head.

The old man flinched, striking her hand away.

"You're mad! All you bitches are mad!" he cried.

The man next to me hissed but did not move.

"I am a man of God! You will be struck down! Struck down for your sins and heresy!" he said and spat on the habit of Sister Vashti.

A heavy hush descended over the crowd. I could feel the tension in the bodies that surrounded me, the desire for action. Sister Vashti only smiled.

"We are the Sisters of Crimoria, Father Griffith, and your death will bring good fortune to us all." Then she turned forward and looked directly at me.

Her cold blue eyes bored into me. The men and women around me stepped back to make room, all except Sister Helena.

"There is another outsider in our midst, one who has partaken in the grapes of Crimoria. Step forward, stranger."

Panic swamped me, drowning me in racing thoughts and a thundering heart. I turned blindly to Sister Helena. She was smiling. Her hand went to mine, the one clutching her habit sleeve and she nodded.

"Don't worry," she said. "Remember my promise."

I did. I did remember it. I knew I had to trust in her then, so I let go, clutching my fists at my sides. Sister Helena leaned in, kissing my cheek, her lips like the brush of butterfly wings.

I went to the old nun, facing her and the priest both.

"My son," Father Griffith begged, reaching out for me.

I did not look at him. I only looked at Sister Vashti, and I saw the corner of her mouth twitch into the briefest of smiles before becoming stern again.

I knew then.

I had passed.

She held her hands out to me and I stepped into them, bending my knees a bit as she kissed one cheek and then the other.

"Brother," she said. "Will you assist me?"

"Yes, Sister," I replied, my whole body trembling—though from fear or excitement, I'll never know.

"Lift up our hallowed sacrifice. Hold him above the mouth of the Eternal Child." The old nun gestured to the post hole that had been left behind by the old scarecrow.

"Please, John, don't do this! You'll be damned! You'll be cast down into Hell with these witches to burn! To burn for all eternity!" the priest howled, struggling to stand then falling back.

I steeled myself and stepped up to him, reaching down and hooking my hands under his armpits. He began to weep then, and I almost stopped. I looked back to the crowd, to Helena. She was watching me, her hands clasped in front of her chest, her eyes wide and filled with reflected moonlight.

I pulled Father Griffith to his feet, and he slumped against me, too weak to even stand. They had to have poisoned him, to have drugged him, I thought as I hauled his left arm around my shoulders to more easily carry him. O'Halloran's voice echoed again: "The food. The food!"

He slapped his free hand feebly against my chest as I took him towards the hole, his feet dragging along the grass.

"Please! Please no, please!" he blubbered and I shut my eyes, gritting my teeth.

I turned us to face the crowd so that he was right over the small hole as I held him steady. The mass of people was a sea of silhouettes whose eyes glinted in the night, still, quiet, waiting. The ground rumbled, the earth lifting in rolling waves around us. The villagers, the nuns, they stood unmoving, riding the waves, watching us.

"We call upon thee, Eternal Child. We beseech thee. Accept our sacrifice. Drink of this man's blood and bless us with thy own—the blood of our shared Mother! We call thee! We, the Daughters of Crimoria! We, your sisters! Accept this humble gift and drink heartily of the most holy Communions!"

Beneath my feet, beneath the feet of all who stood in the small courtyard behind the convent, came a purr. A purr that grew into a growl into a roar until I was deafened.

The ground shuddered and the grape vines shivered. One of the tables crashed to its side as a leg gave way, but the nuns and villagers didn't flinch.

I bit my lip, tasting blood, and looked down at what Sister Vashti had called the 'mouth.' I looked down just in time to see the wooden post shoot out.

Except it wasn't a wooden post.

Yes, it resembled the post I saw before—the one the old scarecrow had been mounted on—except now I could see it for what it really was.

A dark, pulsing appendage with a razor-sharp point that came tearing up through the ground.

Over the cacophony, I heard the priest scream as he was impaled, the eldritch limb piercing him through his pelvis. His bones broke with a crunch, his organs burst softly like the sound of grapes popping, and he was pulled away from me as it pushed him into the air.

His hands flailed, reached for me, his eyes beseeching me as blood coated his lips red. My knees shook and I stumbled away from him, unable to tear my eyes from the sight of the impaled priest. My belly roiled and a sourness crept up my throat.

I bumped into someone, hands gripped my shoulders, a breath tickled my ear.

"I'm here, John. I'm here," Helena whispered.

Father Griffith's head rolled back as his mouth gaped and the point of the stake emerged from between his teeth. Only then did his screams stop. He struggled silently, his hands flapping around his chest, his throat, his head.

The ground shivered again and for the last time as dozens of eyes opened along the horrific limb that held the priest pinned. Eyes with two or three pupils each in an iris as red as wine. The crowd hummed, just one deep note, all together. Buzzing like bees.

The priest began to scream again, his voice muffled by the protruding limb in his throat.

I wrapped my hands tightly over my own mouth, choking back my answering scream. Helena continued to hold me, saying nothing, her body pressed against mine.

The pupils of all those horrible eyes opened, revealing gaping mouths filled with rows and rows of teeth like the maw of a lamprey eel.

"Oh God," I said, swallowing down bile.

"Not God, at least not his God," Helena answered. "The Eternal Child."

The mouth-eyes at the base of the tentacle mewled—a quiet begging—as they sucked at nothing. The priest seemed to deflate, his skin paled to a deathly white, and his arms fell limp to his sides. I imagined the eyes, the ones inside of him, sucking and sucking. Drinking his blood, eating his organs, sating the hunger of the Eternal Child. I could smell it. The reek of blood, of feces as the old priest's bowels let loose.

Shaking, I sunk to my knees. Helena kept a hand on my shoulder. I looked up at her and saw her other hand pressed over her heart, a smile on her lips, as she watched the *thing* feed. For thirty long minutes, it fed. For thirty long minutes, we watched.

When the priest was nothing more than a shrivelled husk, a shadow of the hefty man he had been, the eyes of the Child closed and the ground stilled.

Silence.

The night hung over us and around us like a shroud, the moon was crawling towards the horizon, the eastern sky hinted at the coming dawn.

Movement in the crowd. The villagers turned and left, saying nothing.

The nuns remained in a ring around the impaled priest until the last of the villagers had gone from view. The red-haired Sister Philippa appeared with a small ladder and a bundle of clothing. She set the ladder next to where Father Griffith hung, climbing carefully. At the top, she reached with a short knife and cut the priest's clothes from his body, letting them flutter to the ground.

His body sagged without the internal support of organs and blood, leaving his pale skin to hang in draping folds. Shaking out the black clothing she'd brought, Philippa redressed him, stitching the shirt and trousers closed as she went. The entire farce was completed when she placed an over-sized, wide-brimmed hat over his terror-stricken face, which still faced upwards to the sky, towards the heavens.

When she was finished, all that was left was a scarecrow. A near twin to the one before.

"Blessed be," Sister Vashti intoned.

"Blessed be," replied the sisters.

The gray-haired sister led the procession of nuns away from the vineyard and back into the convent. Sister Helena tugged me up, wrapping an arm around me as she helped me back. I kept my head down, cold and shaking.

She brought me to my room, though I could see the nuns filing into their sanctuary. Some small, curious part of me—perhaps the same part that had made Pandora open the box—wanted to go and join them, to see what their ceremonies were like, but Helena pressed me to lay down.

"You did well," she whispered, pressing a kiss to my sweat slick forehead.

I felt my face flush with pride, joy, disgust... I didn't know. I just nodded and she left, closing the door behind her.

PART V

Aging and Bottling

I woke with a scream caught in my throat, my hands clenching the blankets as I thrashed. Sunlight painted the floor beneath the window with golden swathes, and in the distance, I could hear the sound of women laughing.

I sat up, throwing my legs over the side of the bed, and I rubbed my face with shaking hands. I wanted to cry. I wanted to laugh. Most of all, I wanted to run.

Instead, I pulled out the empty chamber pot from beneath the bed and retched.

When my belly was empty and I had stopped vomiting, I changed into the clean clothes that had been set out for me on the chair closest to my bed. Despite the memories haunting my mind, despite the horror and fear, my belly rumbled, reminding me that biology came first and I was hungry. Opening my room door, I stepped out into the bright hall and made my way to the dining hall. The nuns had already eaten, it seemed, though a single bowl had been left behind, full of porridge.

After finishing it, I went outside to find a miracle.

The nuns danced around the small vineyard and its new guardian, laughing joyously. The vines, which had been thin and drying the day before, were now a lush green and heavy with fully mature grapes where, before, there'd been none at all.

I stumbled forward a few steps.

Grapes as crimson as blood drops, hanging in brilliant clusters from thriving vines laced with pulsing red threads. Threads like veins, winding through the plants, and giving them a burgundy hue. The barefoot, bareheaded nuns danced and danced, weaving through the rows of grapes. Sister Morgan May tumbled out from the vineyard, falling to the grass, laughing, and her hair spread over the ground like a halo.

Sister Vashti stood in front of Father Griffith's body and led three other nuns in song, clapping her hands along to the beat. Sister Philippa and Sister Agatha swung around the side, holding hands and spinning, spinning, spinning in circles until they collapsed.

It was a celebration. Something primal and lustful. Something I didn't feel a part of.

Then Sister Helena Rose emerged from the vines, the top of her habit half open, baring her shoulders. Her toes dug into the soil as she walked towards me, holding a cup in each hand. The sunlight blazed in her hair like a halo, and for a moment, she was a cold, unapproachable pagan Mother Mary.

The spell was broken when she smiled. The wink that followed startled a laugh out of me. I clapped a hand over my mouth.

"Mr. Ainsworth," she said, offering me a cup.

I didn't need to ask what was in it. I drank deeply of the wine, let its warmth, its *life* fill me. I looked over her shoulder to the figure of Father Griffith hanging in the air, his new uniform fluttering in the warm summer breeze.

"This... this sacrifice has to happen every year?" I asked and my voice cracked.

She turned to follow my gaze, sipping from her own cup.

"Yes. Every year, we give the Eternal Child a sacrifice and it sleeps again, gifting us with its own blood."

"Blood," I echoed, looking into my cup.

"Every harvest has its own unique profile," Helena said. "The sacrifices live on. In every cask and bottle. In every sip."

"And when there aren't any convenient strangers?" I asked, wondering who I was drinking then, whose taste I was enjoying.

"A villager will volunteer. Usually someone elderly. Someone close to death already," the nun replied.

"And if Father Griffith hadn't been visiting when I crashed my car? If it had been just me here and now?" My hands were shaking again. I couldn't look at her.

She reached out with her free hand and cupped my face, pulling my gaze up to meet hers.

"The Eternal Child must be sated each and every year upon the anniversary of the Mother's Sacrifice." Her voice was soft, kind, but firm. "But I am glad that it didn't have to be you."

I examined her face. She was blushing and she tried to duck her head as I looked at her. Instead, I tossed my cup to the grass, grabbed her face, and kissed her. I thought she might pull away. Instead, she stepped closer, dropping her hand to my waist. Her lips were soft and she tasted of sweet sun-ripened grapes and the faintest hint of copper.

Too soon, Helena pulled away. Made space between us. Left me with an emptiness and yearning.

"I think you're healed enough to return home, Mr. Ainsworth," she said.

"But, I—" I started, having no idea what I wanted to say.

"This is a convent. You can't stay forever," she continued, her voice gentle.

My heart dropped. Then I looked past her to the scarecrow and felt a chill. The ceremony would happen again next year. And if another stranger didn't come to visit and I was still here...

I nodded. Sister Helena smiled, but this time a sad smile.

"Mr. Winstead will be here soon. He is the one who fixed your car, at least the best he could."

"I—I don't have any money to pay for—"

Helena shook her head.

"It's taken care of. The village, the convent, we all work together."

I stared down at my feet, at a loss.

"Sit with me, Mr. Ainsworth, come," she said, tugging on my hand and I followed her to the side of the convent where there was some shade.

There, we sat in silence, side by side, watching the nuns frolic and celebrate. The mechanic, Mr. Winstead, arrived an hour later in my car. Too soon, too soon he came.

I spotted the rooster plume first, heralding Mr. Winstead's arrival. Next came the eye-piercing glint of sunshine on chrome as my car rolled into view.

Helena meant it when she said the mechanic had tried his best. The hood and windshield had been completely replaced, though the hood was a completely different colour from the rest of the car. Other than that and a few dents in the sides and boot, no one would be able to tell how bad of an accident it had been in.

I stood, brushing the grass from my pants. Helena led the way across the lawn towards where my car was parked. Mr. Winstead pulled himself out of the driver's side and tossed the keys into the air. I caught the keyring easily, recognizing it as my own.

"It's still a bit fiddly, but it'll get you home," the man called, jamming his hands into the pockets of his oil-stained coveralls.

"Thanks, I really owe you one," I said, weakly.

"Think nothing of it." Without waiting for more, the mechanic turned and began making his way down the road back to the village.

Helena placed her hand on my arm, smiling up at me. I felt my heart break.

"Mr. Ainsworth!" Agatha appeared beside me, carrying a hefty basket. Despite the checked cloth covering the contents, I could see three bottle necks poking out. "Open your trunk! You have a special delivery from the Sisters of Crimoria!"

I slid my key into the boot, popping the trunk lid for her. She tucked the basket in carefully.

"Now, Mr. Ainsworth." Agatha placed her fists on her hips. "You make sure to take some breaks now and then. There are some sandwiches and fruit in the basket. And three bottles of our wine to remember us by."

"Thank you, Sister Agatha." My voice caught a little.

"Oh, Mr. Ainsworth. Try not to miss us too much." Agatha stepped forward and wrapped her arms around me, giving me the briefest of hugs, slipping away before I could reciprocate.

She walked away before I could say anything, leaving Helena and me alone by the back of my car. I closed the trunk.

"Can I ever come back?" I asked, staring down at the back tire. "To visit, I mean?"

"I suppose that's up to you, Mr. Ainsworth." Helena took my hand in hers, giving it a gentle squeeze.

I nodded, leaving so many questions unasked. So many things unsaid. She led me around the car to the driver's side door, letting go of my hands to open it for me. By the vineyard, the twelve other nuns gathered to watch, their hands clasped in front of them, smiles on their faces.

I looked back at Helena.

"Drive safe, Mr. Ainsworth," she murmured, standing up on her tiptoes to kiss me lightly on the lips.

It took every ounce of willpower not to reach for her as she stepped back from me, turned, and joined her sisters. It took every ounce still to get into my car and start it, reversing, pulling away down the road and leaving them all—the Sisters of the Crimson Vine, Crimoria Convent, and the Eternal Child—in my rear-view mirror.

Acknowledgements

The Eternal Child bestows blessings upon Timber Ghost Press for giving this novella a home, to the beta-readers – Philippa, Jolie, Angela, and Chris – who spilled their (metaphorical) blood to make the story stronger, to Matthew for his support and constant delivery of tea, and to black cats Poe and Zerg for keeping the vineyard free of mice.

ABOUT THE AUTHOR

P.L. McMillan is a writer whose works have been known to cause rifts in time and space itself...

Well, not quite. But writing often makes her feel that powerful.

With a passion for cosmic horror and sci-fi horror, P.L. McMillan sees every shadow as an entryway to a deeper look into the black heart of the world, meant to be discovered and explored. Infatuated with the works of Shirley Jackson, H.P. Lovecraft, and Ridley Scott, her dream is to create stories of adventure, of chills, of heartbreak, and thrills.

P.L. McMillan lives in Colorado, with her large selection of teas, her husband, and her two chinchillas (Sherlock and Spuds) – all under the supervision of their black cat overlords, Poe and Zerg.

Find her on her website: https://www.plmcmillan.com/ or on Twitter @AuthorPLM.

A Note from Timber Ghost Press

If you enjoyed, *Sisters of the Crimson Vine*, please consider leaving a review on Amazon or Goodreads. Reviews help the author and the press.

If you go to www.timberghostpress.com you can sign up for our newsletter so you can stay up-to-date on all our upcoming titles, plus you'll get informed of new horror flash fiction and poetry featured on our site monthly.

Take care and thanks for reading, *Sisters of the Crimson* Vine by P.L. McMillan.

-Timber Ghost Press

Printed in Great Britain
by Amazon